Praise for the **Amanda Travels** Series

"Fast-paced, spooky, and enough cultural reference to delight both readers and parents."

—*Alex Lyttle, Author of From Ant to Eagle*

"Foster's writing is conversational and easy to read, and young readers will likely find the pages flying by."

—*Quill & Quire*

"A mysterious travel adventure with a brave, inquisitive, compassionate heroine. This is a fast-paced, fun read! Amanda will take you on a wonderful, visual, descriptive adventure."

—*Author PJ Sarah Collins & Daughter, Elena Collins, Age 11*

"Young readers will have great fun travelling alongside Amanda Ross in this fast-paced mystery that will keep readers guessing until the very last chapter."

—*Jan L. Coates, Author, Finalist - Governor General's Literary Awards*

"A charming and fast-paced story that will delight its young audience as Amanda and Leah travel along the historic Danube River to deliver a very unique and mysterious violin."

—*Suzanne de Montigny, Author*

"There is A LOT of action packed into this little book!"

—*Mother Daughter Reviews*

Book of the Month: "Amanda in England: a delightful romp through modern-day London. Recommended for readers in late elementary school or for anyone who loves solving playful mysteries that do not reveal their secrets easily."

—*Long and Short Reviews*

"I love how Ms. Foster puts the reader right in the action and kids get to learn about the exciting places Amanda goes."

—*This Kid Reviews Books*

The **Amanda Travels** Series:

Amanda in Arabia: The Perfume Flask

Amanda in Spain: The Girl in the Painting

Amanda in England: The Missing Novel

Amanda in Alberta: The Writing on the Stone

Amanda on the Danube: The Sounds of Music

AMANDA
IN
NEW MEXICO
GHOSTS IN THE WIND

DARLENE FOSTER

central
avenue

2017

Published by Central Avenue Publishing, an imprint of Central Avenue Marketing Ltd.
www.centralavenuepublishing.com

Published in Canada
Printed in United States of America

Lexile® measure: 600L

1. JUVENILE FICTION/Travel 2. JUVENILE FICTION / People & Places - America

Library and Archives Canada Cataloguing in Publication

Foster, Darlene, author
      Amanda in New Mexico : ghosts in the wind / Darlene Foster.

(Amanda travels ; 6)
Issued in print and electronic formats.
ISBN 978-1-77168-120-9 (softcover).--ISBN 978-1-77168-121-6 (EPUB).--
ISBN 978-1-77168-122-3 (Kindle)

      I. Title.

PS8611.O7883A7 2017   jC813'.6   C2017-900421-2
                                               C2017-900422-0

To Todd and Marcelle,
My reason for being.

1

AMANDA TRIED TO SHOUT. NOTHING CAME OUT OF HER mouth. Something tugged at the covers. Her breaths came in short gasps as she clutched the blanket tight to her pounding heart.

"Amanda, what are you doing? You're completely covered by your duvet."

She threw back the quilt when she heard her mother's voice. "I—I don't know. It felt like something scary was in the room."

"It's just a bad dream." Mrs. Ross stroked her daughter's short, sweaty hair. "Perhaps you should stop reading scary novels. Now, go get in the shower or you'll be late for school."

"Yikes! Look at the time." Amanda jumped out of bed and was nearly at the bathroom door when she remembered something. "Do you have the money, Mom? Today is the last day to pay for the school trip to New Mexico."

"The cheque is in your backpack with your homework and lunch. Now make it snappy or you'll miss the bus." Her mom looked at her watch and left the room.

After a quick breakfast, Mr. Ross handed Amanda her backpack. "The cheque for your school trip to Mexico is in here, make sure you don't lose it."

"Dad, how many times do I have to tell you, I'm going to *New* Mexico, not Mexico." She shook her head and sighed. "New Mexico is a state in the United States. Mexico is a whole country."

"Sorry." Don Ross shrugged. "I'm an accountant, not a geographer, or world traveller like you."

"I'm just glad you're not flying the plane." She glanced out the window. "Oh no! Here comes the bus."

Amanda ran down the street to the waiting school bus. "Thanks," she said to the smiling driver. Out of breath, she slid into the empty seat beside Cleo.

"Whew, you cut that close," said her friend.

"Whatever. Mr. Kozak always waits for me." Amanda flapped her hand. "Did you bring your money for the school trip?"

"Yup!" Cleo patted her backpack. "I'm not missing this for the world."

💀 💀 💀

A few weeks later, at the airport in Albuquerque, New Mexico, a minibus waited for the ten grade six students from Calgary's Guy Weadick Elementary.

"That sun sure is bright." Amanda squinted and shaded her eyes with her hand. "Will it be this hot where we're going, Mr. Samson?"

The chubby art teacher threw another suitcase in the back of the vehicle. "We're going to Taos, which is in the mountains, so it won't be hot." He wiped the sweat off his forehead with the back of his hand. "Now, everybody, please get on board."

Amanda pulled her friend along. "Let's get a seat at the front so we can see everything."

Cleo hesitated. "I'm not sure." Her face paled and her lips trembled. She brushed her curly red hair from her eyes.

"What do you mean?" Amanda knit her brow. "Don't you feel well?"

Cleo looked down. "I—I wish I was at home. I just got an awful feeling. I think something bad is going to happen on this trip."

Amanda gave her a reassuring hug. "It will be fine. You'll see. We'll have lots of fun. You probably just haven't been away from home before." She helped Cleo onto the bus. "I'll make sure you'll be OK," Amanda said as they settled into seats right behind Mr. Samson.

"Amanda, do you believe in ghosts?" asked Cleo.

"No, I don't," replied Amanda. "Do you?"

Cleo leaned over and whispered, "I saw a ghost once, at my grandmother's old house."

Amanda's head shot up. "No way!"

"Yes, way. It scared me so much I've never been back

for a sleepover." Cleo bit at the skin beside her thumb-nail.

"Well, you're sharing a room with me. I promise to keep all ghosts away," Amanda said with a comforting smile. She wasn't sure what to make of this new information from her friend.

☠ ☠ ☠

They arrived at the town of Taos late in the afternoon. At the end of a quiet cobblestone road, the bus stopped at a three-story, terracotta house, tucked in between tall fir trees. The building looked like it had been created out of modelling clay. Colourful clay roosters looked down on them from the flat roof.

Amanda had done some research before the trip. She knew the house and other buildings on the property were originally built in the early 1900s by Mable Dodge Luhan. The wealthy woman invited artists and writers to stay there. Nowadays it was used for artists' retreats, conferences and school visits. Each room in the big house was named after a famous person who had once stayed there. Amanda and Cleo were given Spud's Room on the main floor.

Amanda opened the door of their room and peered in. "This is so sweet. Look, we get our own bathroom and a cool fireplace."

"The furniture looks old and spooky," said Cleo as she

claimed one of the twin beds by placing her suitcase on it.

"That's the point. It looks just like it did all those years ago when famous people stayed here." Amanda ran her hand over a green leather chair. "I love it!"

A tall, dark-haired woman poked her head in the door. "Is your room all right?" asked Ms. Bowler, the grade six teacher.

"It's super!" Amanda's eyes sparkled.

"This was Spud Johnson's room. He was Mable Lohan's private secretary and a writer himself. He published a magazine called *The Laughing Horse* and printed it on a small handheld printing press. You can see the press on display in the living room."

"That is so awesome," said Amanda. "Where are you staying, Ms. Bowler?"

"I'm staying in the Gate House Cottage with the other teachers. We each have our own room. It's very cozy."

"Are there any ghosts here?" asked Cleo.

Ms. Bowler ruffled Cleo's curly red hair. "No, sweetie, there are no ghosts. Just great vibes from talented authors and artists. We are very lucky to be able to stay here. Remember, you were all picked for this trip because you like to write, paint or take pictures. Don't forget to log onto *Kidblog* so you can write about your experiences in New Mexico. You can start by writing about the bus trip here or your first impressions of the house and your room." The teacher glanced around. "Once you've freshened up, come downstairs to the dining room. The cook has prepared a nice meal for us."

"Thanks, Ms. Bowler. I can't wait to write about this place. We'll be down soon."

Amanda began to put her things in a drawer. "You can have the closet." She looked over at her friend.

Cleo stood in front of the open closet door, shivering like someone who had been soaked with a garden hose in January.

2

"WHAT IS IT?" AMANDA MOVED OVER TO CLEO AND PEERED into the empty closet.

"I—I thought I saw someone when I—I opened the door," Cleo stammered.

"There's nothing in here except hangers." Amanda swiped her hand around the inside. "Oh, and these two white bathrobes hanging at the end. Maybe they moved when the door swung open."

"Maybe." Cleo swallowed and looked down.

Amanda reached for Cleo's hand. "Let's go downstairs and get something to eat. We can unpack later. Besides, I'm starved."

Amanda led the way to the dining room on the lower level where they met the other students. The room felt warm and cozy. In the centre of the red and black tiled floor sat a heavy oak table with high-backed chairs surrounding it. Several smaller tables, each set for four, stood in the corners of the room. Vibrant art decorated the walls. French doors led out to a spacious courtyard with more tables and chairs.

Amanda looked up. The ceiling, painted with diagonal stripes of red, black and white between the wood beams, looked like a Navajo rug. A black, wrought-iron chandelier hung from the centre.

A woman, in a long white apron and a floppy chef's hat, greeted the children. "The kitchen and dining room are exactly as they were over a hundred years ago. Mrs. Luhan and her husband, Tony, entertained their many notable guests here. This room was often jam-packed. I'm Audrey, by the way, and will be your cook, hostess and general know-it-all during your stay. Anything you want to know, I'll do my dang best to answer for you young folk." She winked at Amanda and Cleo.

Amanda immediately loved Audrey's southern accent and warm personality.

"Come, have a look at the kitchen, and then you all can eat." Audrey motioned for the children to follow her.

The smell of roast chicken made Amanda even hungrier. Along one side of the kitchen, a dark wood cupboard with a brightly tiled counter top held a sink, toaster, coffee machine and a large spice rack. The windowsill, lined with cheerful red geraniums and herbs in blue pots, looked out into the garden. A massive stainless steel stove with two ovens rested against another wall. Beside it, a large rack held stainless steel pots, bowls and utensils. A butcher's block stood in the middle of the room, bearing platters piled high with chicken, dumplings, mashed potatoes, green beans and bright orange carrots.

"Most everything we eat here is from our garden, and is grown organically," said Audrey. "So, grab a plate and help yerselves."

"This is so good, isn't it?" Amanda took another bite of roast chicken and glanced at Cleo. She was enjoying the hearty meal, her face no longer pale. Amanda hoped she had heard the last of ghosts.

Later that evening, after unpacking, Cleo soaked in a bubble bath. Amanda took out her tablet and wrote an article on *Kidblog* about her impressions of New Mexico so far. Then she sent an email to her parents and one to her friend Leah, in England. She really wished Leah could be here with her on this trip as they always had so much fun when they travelled together. She wondered what her friend would think of Cleo's phasmophobia, or fear of ghosts. Amanda had been studying phobias recently and kept a notebook with a list of weird dreads.

💀 💀 💀

After tasty breakfast burritos the next morning, the children went downtown to the Governor Bent Museum. A friendly man called George took them through the dusty old museum while explaining the history of the area. There was a stuffed eight-legged lamb that intrigued the boys. Some stopped to make sketches while others took pictures.

"This museum was the home of Governor Charles Bent who served as the first United States territorial governor of New Mexico," described George. "He lived in this house with his family and died here in this very room in 1847." He pointed to a bricked-up oval hole in the wall. "It was through this opening his wife and children escaped to the house next door when the local Mexicans and Indians broke into their home and killed the governor."

George picked up a piece of paper and waved it in front of the students. "This is a report of the incident in the words of Teresina Bent, his daughter, who witnessed it at the tender age of five. I have photocopies for any of you who would like to read it."

Amanda's hand shot up. "I would like a copy, please. Why did they kill him?"

"They were unhappy about having an Anglo-American rule the territory their people had lived in for many centuries."

"How sad," said Amanda. She took a copy of the story from George.

"Do you want one?" she asked Cleo.

"No, thanks."

When the group stopped at a café for a milkshake, Amanda began to read the article.

"I can't believe this. This poor little girl saw her father murdered right in front of her and the whole family!"

Amanda read out loud from the piece of paper:

"*We were in bed when the Mexicans and Indians came to the house breaking doors. Some of them were on top of the roof, so we got up and Father stepped to the porch, asking them what they wanted and they answered him, we want your head, Gringo, we do not want for any of you gringos to govern us, as we have come to kill you.*'"

Cleo clapped her hands over her ears. "Oh, please, don't read any more of that awful story."

Amanda folded the paper in half and put it in her backpack. "I'm sorry, Cleo. At least we know his wife and children were spared. Teresina wrote this when she was a married woman. It seems they had a different way of saying things back then."

"Yes, they did. Let's go for a walk around the town," suggested Ms. Bowler. "There are some cute shops if you're looking for souvenirs to take home."

Amanda finished her milkshake with a slurp and jumped up. "I'm into that!"

The students had fun looking in the adobe style shops filled with unique local crafts. Amanda bought herself a tiny, terracotta, good luck pig called a *chanchito* and a beaded, multi-coloured gecko pin for her mom at a shop called *Earth and Spirit Gallery*. In a small, building that used to be the town jail, they sampled handmade chocolates.

"It's hard to think this place used to be a jail," said Amanda as she swallowed a tasty coconut truffle. She picked up a package of spooky skull-shaped sugar candies painted with bright skeleton faces.

"These are very popular for the Day of the Dead which is coming up soon," said the sales clerk.

Amanda wanted to ask more about the Day of the Dead but the other students had left the shop already. She quickly paid for the candies.

Once she caught up with the others, Amanda noticed a street sign which read, Teresina Lane. "Do you think this street is named after Teresina Bent?"

"I believe so," replied Ms. Bowler.

A breeze sent a shiver through Amanda. She thought of how terrified the little girl must have been on that horrible night her father was killed.

3

"Ms. Bowler, where are we going this afternoon?"

"We're going to visit a *hacienda*, Amanda." Ms. Bowler adjusted her glasses.

"What's that?" asked a boy named Caleb as he fiddled with his camera lens.

"It's the main house on a ranch or large estate." The teacher sounded like she was quoting from a dictionary. "The one we are going to is *Hacienda de los Martinez*. It has been restored into a museum depicting how the Spanish settlers lived here two hundred years ago. There'll be great photo opportunities for you." Ms. Bowler nodded at Caleb.

The *hacienda* was a short bus ride from the town centre. The flat roofed, windowless clay building stood lonely in the middle of a dry field. Two large, beehive shaped, terracotta mud ovens sat outside the door. The teacher explained the ovens, called *hornos,* were used to bake the daily bread.

Beside the massive wooden door, a post with a sign nailed to it stood guard. Amanda giggled when she read what was under the picture of a donkey:

MULE PARKING ONLY.
ALL OTHERS TOWED AWAY.

She snapped a picture.

The group followed Ms. Bowler through the door which opened into a square courtyard. The teacher handed out a map of the hacienda to each student. "The people who lived here spent most of their time outdoors. This *placita* or courtyard would have been a hive of activity. Imagine the inhabitants processing wool and leather, cooking and baking, mending equipment and other farm activities. These rooms surrounding the courtyard would have been used only in bad weather." She pointed around. "You have an hour to explore the rooms on your own. Don't forget to take pictures, make sketches and jot down notes. Any questions?"

Amanda put up her hand. "Why is the front door so huge?"

"The large, heavy door was built so that in the event of an attack, the wagons and livestock could be brought into the courtyard for protection. Notice there are no windows on the outside and the walls are two feet thick. The *hacienda* was considered a refuge for the family and their neighbours."

Amanda glanced at an old stone well in one corner and a donkey cart in another. "Where should we start?"

she asked Cleo.

"Let's start here." Cleo pointed on the map. "Please stay close to me though; it's spooky here. I have a bad feeling." Cleo tugged at the curls escaping from her baseball cap as she squinted.

"Don't be silly. This was just a family's home." Amanda entered the dim room called a *sala* and read the explanation on the map. "It says here this was the main living area."

"There isn't much in here," Cleo said, scanning the packed-earth floor.

"I guess they didn't have much furniture. Look, the beds are above the stove. That would keep them warm." Amanda stroked a carved chest. "I wonder what they kept in here." She tried to open it but it seemed locked.

A bright light flashed.

Cleo screamed.

Amanda whirled around.

Caleb grinned from ear-to-ear. "Got you!" He held up his camera.

"Don't do that! Look how you frightened Cleo." Amanda glared at the boy.

Cleo trembled. Her freckles stood out on her pale face. Amanda steered her out into the sunlight.

"Maybe we shouldn't go into any more rooms," said Cleo.

Amanda groaned. "But I really want to see more. Cleo,

there are no ghosts or anything like that." She crossed her arms. "It was just a camera flash."

Cleo looked down and chewed her thumbnail.

Amanda sighed. "I know, you can wait by the well if you want. Why don't you draw some sketches of the courtyard while I look in the rest of the rooms?"

Cleo pulled her sketchbook from her backpack. "OK, good idea."

Amanda followed the map and looked in the chapel, granary, kitchen, and trade room. She joined Caleb and some of the others in the *sala grande*.

"This is the only room with a wood floor in the *hacienda*. It was made especially for Spanish dance parties called *fandangos*," explained a guide wearing a brightly coloured full skirt, a blouse with puffy sleeves and an apron. She opened a trunk. "You can try on some of clothes that were worn at the time."

Amanda placed a *sombrero* on her head. It was way too big and slipped over her ears. She laughed as Caleb took her picture. Then he flung a colourful striped *serape* over his shoulder and danced around.

"Do you think you're at a *fandango*?" said Amanda as she took his picture.

A shadow appeared on the wall. They both turned to see what caused it. No one was there. An awful toilet smell filled the room. Amanda looked at Caleb. He shrugged his shoulders.

The guide returned and Amanda asked, "Where were the bathrooms?"

"We get asked that a lot." The guide chuckled as she placed an embroidered shawl around her shoulders. "The truth is, there weren't any! Here, in the early 1800s, folks either used chamber pots or they went outside to relieve themselves. Outhouses didn't become common until the late nineteenth century. Bathing was almost unheard of and lice were prevalent."

"Yuck, they must have been awfully smelly." Amanda wrinkled her nose and scratched her arm.

Caleb sniffed. "Like you."

Amanda punched his shoulder. "More like you."

They stepped outside and Amanda noticed students going through a narrow stone corridor. Amanda called over to Cleo. "Are you OK? We're going through there." She pointed to the passageway.

Cleo looked up from her sketch pad and waved. "I'm good. You go ahead."

Once through the opening, they entered a smaller courtyard with more rooms surrounding it. Doors led into a blacksmith's shop and weaving room.

Amanda stood in front of a door the map showed as the *Santos Display Room*. "What's in here?"

Along with Caleb and a couple of other students, she entered the dimly-lit room containing glass cabinets filled with pictures and statues of various saints. A sign explained how the families in Spanish America always kept a shrine to a saint in their homes. The shrine often held *Milagros,* tiny silver shapes attached to statues of the saints. There were legs for people who couldn't walk, eyes for those who had bad eyesight and animal figures to wish a farmer a productive year with his flock. Amanda was fascinated as she peered through the glass at small objects stuck on the figures.

She looked up and gasped. At the end of the narrow room stood a life-sized skeleton of a woman riding in a wooden cart. Amanda, heart beating, crept closer to the scary figure wearing a scraggly white wig and a long dark robe. She carried a scythe in one hand and a globe in the other. On the wall beside the figure, a plaque told of *Doña Sebastiana*, the female saint of death, or *Santa Muerte*. During the Holy Week procession at Easter, this female Grim Reaper was rolled out in her death cart and transported through the town. Parents would point her out and tell the children if they did not behave, *Doña Sebastiana* would come for them.

Amanda gulped and peered more closely at the horrible figure. She couldn't understand why parents would want to scare their children like that. 'Imagine the nightmares!' Amanda thought.

Just then, everything went black. Something brushed Amanda's shoulder. She froze.

"Caleb," she whispered. "Is that you?"

There was no answer.

A cold breeze passed over her.

4

AMANDA FELT HER WAY TO THE DOOR AND PUSHED IT OPEN. She didn't realize she had been holding her breath until she stumbled into the bright sunshine.

As she took a gulp of fresh air, she noticed Caleb chatting and laughing with the other boys. "If that was your idea of a joke, it wasn't funny."

Caleb stared at her. "What're you talking about?"

"You switched off the lights and left me alone in there."

"Uh, no way. The lights were on when I left. I thought you were right behind me. I wasn't staying in there with that creepy skeleton thing."

Mr. Samson shouted, "It's time to go now. Finish what you're doing and meet at the front gate in five minutes."

Still shaking, Amanda found Cleo by the well and sat down beside her. Cleo showed her a sketch of the donkey cart.

"That's very good," said Amanda as the sketchbook shook in her hand.

"Thanks." Cleo looked up at her. "Are you all right? You look a bit funny."

"I'm fine. Just a bit hungry, that's all." She decided it would be best not to tell her ghost-believing friend what had just happened.

Amanda looked at Cleo's picture again. Beside the donkey cart stood a young girl in a long, flowing white dress. She looked transparent.

"Who's this girl?"

"I don't know. She just walked into my scene while I was drawing. She was so pretty, I decided to include her."

"Um, she is very beautiful." Amanda narrowed her eyes. 'Is this girl real or is Cleo imagining things? This day is just getting too weird.' She sighed and picked up Cleo's backpack. "We better get on the bus." Amanda scanned the courtyard once more before going through the big door. She swore someone was watching them.

💀 💀 💀

Back at the house, they had some free time to relax before dinner.

Amanda peered out the window. "It's still nice outside. I'd like to explore the grounds before the sun sets. Want to come?"

Cleo looked up from the book she was reading. "No, thanks, I think I'll stay here."

Amanda passed through the main sitting room, stopping to look at some of the art on the walls. She examined the printing press that Spud Johnson used to print his magazine, *The Laughing Horse*.

Audrey entered the room. "That there machine is quite different from how magazines are printed these days. It's all done with computers now, I suppose. Did you have a good day?"

"Oh, yes. It was so interesting. Audrey, are there any ghosts around here?"

Audrey scratched her head. "Well, there are those folks who believe there are ghosts in these parts. Me? I'm not so sure. In the old days, many people came to an untimely end here. It was quite wild and dangerous. So you never know." She gave Amanda a reassuring pat on the shoulder. "I wouldn't concern myself with it if I were you. I've never heard of any old ghosts hurting someone anyways."

"Thanks, Audrey. I'm going to have a look around outside."

"Don't be long now. We'll be eating soon."

The spacious grounds, scattered with flower gardens and adobe buildings, had lots of nooks and crannies to explore. Amanda found a statue of St. Francis of Assisi tucked in among pine trees and shrubs. Surrounded by clay birds and small animals, the kind monk held out a bowl of water. Her great aunt had a similar statue in her garden. Aunt Mary had explained that St. Francis was the patron saint of animals.

A rustle in the shrubs startled Amanda.

"Don't disturb me."

Amanda gulped. "Who said that?"

She looked around her. No one was there.

"Leave me alone." The harsh whisper sounded closer.

Her stomach tightened. Amanda dashed into a wooded area. She raced down a path not knowing or caring where she was going. Spooky shadows danced along the path. She looked left and right, not sure where to go next. A cold breeze pushed her forward.

She scurried around a corner into a clearing, bending over to catch her breath. When she looked up, several birdhouses sitting on top of poles stared down at her. Different than any she had seen before, they reminded her of mini condominiums. One had six floors, with holes for eight feathered residents on each floor. She wanted to stay and examine the interesting birdhouses but she couldn't shake the uncomfortable feeling that someone or something was following her.

A twig snapped.

Amanda jumped.

Holding back a scream, she fled out of the bird village. She spotted a terracotta gate with a small bell hanging from the top. Running through the opening, she saw a building with a set of mud steps leading up to a blue door. Amanda needed to get in that door, to safety. She barely noticed the sombre-faced native woman with shoulder-length black hair painted on the side of the stairs.

Amanda bolted up the steps, two at a time, the menacing cool breeze at her heels the whole way. She yanked the handle. The door wouldn't budge. Her mouth went dry. Her heart pounded loud in her ears. She felt trapped.

'Is this a bad dream?' she wondered.

Convinced someone was behind her, Amanda stood still. Without turning around she said in a slow firm voice, "I don't know who you are, or what you want. Just go away and leave...me...alone!"

"Amanda, who are you talking to?"

She spun around to see Caleb standing at the bottom of the steps with his hands on his hips.

"Have you lost your mind? Only crazy people talk to themselves."

Amanda felt her cheeks get hot. "I—I thought someone was chasing me."

Caleb laughed. "Maybe it was *Doña Sebastiana* coming to get you. Come on down. It's time to eat. I was sent to find you." He walked part way up the stairs and reached out his hand to help her down. "Are you OK? You're shaking. You look like you just saw a ghost."

"Yeah, I'm fine. It just got dark and spooky out here." Amanda felt her ears turn red and she let go of his hand. "I wonder what we're having for supper tonight. I'm starved." She sprinted ahead.

5

THE SUN SHONE BRIGHTLY THE NEXT MORNING AS THE noisy group of students got on the bus.

Cleo joined Amanda. "I'm sorry I've been such a downer on this trip. I don't know why I've been so silly." She pulled her cap down over her red curls and smiled.

"No worries." Amanda grinned back at her friend, pleased that she finally seemed happy. "This place is so fascinating. Let's just go have fun."

"Absolutely!"

Sometimes, Cleo seemed like two different people.

Amanda reached into her backpack. "Now, what's on the agenda for today?" She pulled out the schedule the teacher had given them. "I see we're going to an old church called Saint Francis of Assisi in the historic Ranchos Plaza. According to this, it is one of the most photographed Spanish Colonial churches in the U.S.A. Glad I brought my camera."

"And I'm glad I brought my sketch pad," said Cleo.

"There is a Saint Francis statue in the gardens where we're staying. He's obviously popular around here."

Amanda continued to read. "It also says there is a mystery painting at the church. I wonder what a 'mystery painting' is?"

"As long as you girls don't get spooked by it." Caleb leaned over the back of the seat in front of them.

"We're more likely to get spooked by you and your scary face." Amanda rolled her eyes at him.

"Ha, ha. You're sooo funny!" Caleb turned back around.

Cleo whispered, "I think he likes you."

"I don't think so. Besides, he can be so annoying. I've known Caleb since kindergarten. We're just friends."

"Not like me. I've only been at this school for a few months now." Cleo looked a bit sad again.

"Well, I feel like I've known you for a long time." Amanda patted her hand. She realized she really didn't know that much about Cleo except that she used to live in another province before she moved to Calgary. Amanda had never been invited around to her house or even met her parents.

❀ ❀ ❀

The church was quite different from the ornate cathedrals Amanda saw on her travels in Europe. Simple and plain, it was covered in smooth rust-coloured mud like everything else in the area. Three white crosses stood out against the clear blue sky, one over the doorway and one on top of a bell tower flanking each side. A thick mud fence surrounded the building.

A hush fell over the usually noisy students as they entered the peaceful courtyard through an archway adorned with another white cross. A statue of St. Francis greeted the visitors. In the centre of the stone pathway leading to the white doors of the church stood a large cross with the words, *San Francisco de Assis*.

The clicking of cameras broke the silence.

"OK, everyone, we are allowed to have a quick look inside the church but you are not allowed to take pictures inside," Ms. Bowler announced.

Dozens of fresh lilies decorated the church. Elaborate paintings of biblical scenes in heavy wooden frames covered the walls. Large timber beams held up the ceiling.

Amanda's nose itched from the strong scent of the lilies. Eager to leave the dark church, she returned to the bright courtyard where she spotted Caleb taking pictures around the side of the building.

"Anything interesting?"

"I wonder how they get the walls so smooth. What I really want is to get a closer look at those cool buildings over there." He pointed to some ruins. "Wanna come with me?"

Amanda nodded and followed Caleb out of the gate.

The derelict buildings seemed to have been deserted for some time. Most of the mud had fallen off, revealing the adobe bricks underneath. The roofs sagged. Jagged ends of rotted wood beams stuck out the sides. The dark, open spaces of absent doors and windows looked like missing teeth. Amanda and Caleb crunched through the dry, overgrown weeds to get a closer look.

Amanda patted the rough bricks. "I wonder who used to live in these buildings."

Caleb concentrated on taking pictures. He turned on his flash and pointed the camera through a partially boarded up window.

"Is there anything in there?" Amanda stood on tiptoe to peer inside but only saw darkness.

"Caleb! Amanda! Over here. It's time to see the mystery painting. Hurry up!" Ms. Bowler called from a doorway.

Caleb looked at his last picture and gulped.

"What is it?" asked Amanda.

"Nothing. It's nothing." Caleb put his camera back in the case hanging from his neck. "We can't miss seeing the Mystery Painting." He made quotation marks with his index fingers.

They approached a building where the other students waited outside a wooden door decorated with carvings of two monks. A cross painted in the middle split in two when the door opened. The students entered and sat in folding chairs facing a curtain. A woman with a Spanish accent introduced herself as Maria.

"What you are about to see is unexplainable. It is a painting called *The Shadow of the Cross* done by a Canadian artist, Henri Ault, in 1896. This is our greatest treasure. It is a life-size picture of our Lord standing by the Sea of Galilee. This is what it looks like with the lights on." She pulled the curtain open to reveal a painting of Jesus wearing a brown robe and a blue shawl over his shoulders, surrounded by faint white clouds on a light blue sky.

Amanda thought it was a very nice painting and felt proud that a fellow Canadian painted it.

Maria continued, "Now I will turn out the lights so you can see how the painting changes. There is nothing to be frightened of."

The lights went out. The children gasped. Immediately the once bright painting turned dark and stormy. The sea and sky glowed. The shadowy black figure looked 3D. A cross stood over his left shoulder and a halo circled above his head. In one corner of the choppy sea, the bow of a small boat emerged.

Maria put the lights back on and the picture appeared as it was before.

Amanda's hand shot up. "How can it change like that? Did he use special paint?"

"No one seems to know," answered Maria. "That is the mystery."

"They must have put radium in the paint," Caleb said.

"That is a very good guess, except that it was painted before radium was discovered. Scientists have tested the paint and cannot find an answer as to why this happens. Would you like to see it again?"

Amanda looked over at her roommate. Cleo sat very still, staring with wide eyes at the painting. "Do you want to leave, Cleo?"

6.

CLEO DIDN'T ANSWER. AMANDA TOUCHED HER SHOULDER.

"Cleo, let's leave, OK?"

The young girl jerked and looked at Amanda as if woken from a dream. "What did you say?"

"I'm going outside. Do you want to come with me?" Amanda stood up.

"Sure."

Some of the students stayed behind to see the changes in the fascinating painting again.

Caleb joined Amanda and Cleo outside. "That was cool. There has to be another explanation, though. It's highly unlikely it's magic."

"Well...you never know," said Amanda.

Cleo rubbed her forehead. "I'm going to wait in the bus. I feel a bit dizzy." She walked toward the bus parked on the road beside the churchyard.

"What's with her?" Caleb asked.

"She's OK." Amanda glanced in Cleo's direction and sighed. "She just gets frightened easily."

"Well, I think she's weird." Caleb flicked through his

pictures. "Hey, um, what do you think this is?" He handed his camera to Amanda.

Amanda squinted at the small screen. "I'm not sure. It could be bones, maybe even a skeleton." She shuddered and handed back the camera. "Is this the picture you took inside the old building?"

"Yup."

Maria and the rest of the children came out to join them.

"Who used to live in those falling-down buildings over there?" Amanda pointed in the direction of the old houses.

Maria replied, "A long time ago those buildings were military barracks. They haven't been used for ages. For some reason, many people stay away from them. There have been rumours, but there always are around here."

"What kind of rumours?"

Maria shrugged. "Oh, nothing really. Any other questions?"

Caleb put up his hand. "How do they make the outside of the church so smooth?"

"Every year hundreds of volunteers from the area smooth clay mud, straw and water over the church to resurface its tens of thousands of adobe bricks. It is so beautiful when it is finished. It sparkles like a jewel in the sun." Maria beamed. "I am pleased you like our church."

Ms. Bowler scanned the area. "Where is Cleo?"

"She went back to the bus," said Amanda. "She wasn't feeling well."

The teacher wrinkled her brow. "I was just at the bus and she wasn't th—"

A scream pierced the air.

"It's coming from over there!" Caleb pointed to the deserted buildings. He ran toward the sound.

Amanda felt sick to her stomach. She watched Caleb put his feet on the exposed bricks as he attempted to climb up to a window.

"Caleb!" Ms. Bowler shouted. "Don't go in there. It could be dangerous."

"What is happening, *Señora*?" asked Maria. An elderly priest followed closely behind her.

"One of the students is missing. We just heard a scream coming from that building." Ms. Bowler pointed.

"Oh, no!" Maria placed a trembling hand on her chest.

The priest put one hand on her shoulder. He pulled out a cell phone from his robe's pocket with the other hand and called emergency services.

Caleb ignored his teacher and Maria. With one hand grasping the windowsill, he ripped at a loose board. He peered into the dark room.

"Be careful." Amanda came up behind him. "What can you see?"

"Nothing. It's very dark in here. And a bit stinky."

"What are these kids doing here?" A man in a denim

jacket and a straw cowboy hat yelled as he came around the back of the building. "You there! Get away from that window. It's dangerous. That wall could give way at any time." He shook his head and pulled Caleb away from the window.

Ms. Bowler came up to the man's side. "I'm so sorry." She turned to Caleb, her eyes flashing. "I told you to stay back."

A sorrowful moan came from inside.

"I—I think Cleo might be in that house." Amanda winced when she thought of what else might be in there.

"You should really keep better track of these kids." The man glared at Ms. Bowler. "Let me take a look." He walked around to the side of the building and pulled open a shabby door.

A couple of minutes later he came out carrying a limp Cleo. "How the heck did she get in there anyway?" He scowled.

Just then a police car and an ambulance pulled into the parking area.

"What's going on, Jim?" asked the police officer.

"I found this young girl in the old building. How many times have I said not to let people wander around here? She seems to have passed out. Better get her checked out." Jim handed Cleo over to the ambulance attendants.

A flustered Ms. Bowler herded the curious students onto the bus.

"May I stay with Cleo?" Amanda asked. "She might want to see a familiar face when she comes to."

The teacher ran her hands through her hair. "Yes, yes, I guess that would be fine. Just be careful. We can't have anything else happen."

Amanda squeezed past Maria and the priest to get to Cleo, lying on a stretcher. She opened her eyes and looked around in a daze.

"It's all right, Cleo. I'm here." Amanda bent over her friend.

Cleo murmured, "B-bones. There were bones everywhere. It was so s-scary." Then she jerked her head from left to right. "The girl. Where is the girl?"

7

"WHAT GIRL? WHAT ARE YOU TALKING ABOUT, CLEO?"

"The girl that was with me in the old building." Amanda leaned closer to hear Cleo whisper. "You know, the one I saw at the *hacienda*."

The ambulance attendant approached them. "We're ready to put your friend in the ambulance and take her to the hospital."

"No!" Cleo bolted upright, almost bumping her head against Amanda's. "I'm not going to a hospital again!" She swung her legs over the side of the stretcher. "I feel better now. I want to go back on the bus with the others."

"I'm not sure that is a good idea." The attendant placed his hands on her shoulders.

"I'm all right. Amanda, help me up." Cleo reached out her hand.

Amanda took hold of it and pulled her up.

"See, I can stand just fine." Cleo took a few wobbly steps. "Amanda will help me to the bus."

The ambulance attendant shook his head. "Here, I'll help you." He put his arm around her shoulder and walked her toward the waiting bus.

At the bus, Cleo thanked the attendant. Everyone cheered when she got on. Ms. Bowler insisted she sit beside her on the front seat.

Amanda wondered, 'Why was Cleo so adamant about not going to the hospital? And, who was this girl that was with her?'

💀 💀 💀

After lunch, Mr. Samson organized a walk into town. Ms. Bowler stayed behind with Cleo and a couple of others who preferred not to go. Amanda was glad she didn't have to keep an eye on Cleo.

Caleb walked up beside her. "How did Cleo get in that building anyway? There is something totally weird about that girl."

Amanda nodded her head but didn't say anything.

"Take a look at those sculptures!" Amanda pointed to bronze statues scattered around a square. "At first glance, this one looks like a face. When you look at it a second time, it appears to be three dark figures in hooded cloaks. It all depends on how you look at it."

Caleb pulled out his camera. "Wow, these sculptures are really cool."

Amanda noticed various paintings on display in the square. In one corner, an artist sat on a stump hunched over a small piece of paper. She walked over and watched as he applied bright orange to the heavy paper. He looked up at her and smiled. Paintings pinned onto a piece of cardboard leaned against a chair. She stepped closer and observed an eagle against a bright orange sun, a buffalo on a purple background and next to it, a wolf with a feather in his mouth.

"I like your paintings," said Amanda.

"Thank you. They represent animals from my people's folklore. I live at the *pueblo* up the road. Have you been there?"

"Not yet. We're going tomorrow."

"My people have lived there for a thousand years. We still live as they did."

He continued painting until a single vibrant dragonfly appeared. He finished it with a tall weed on one side.

"Do you like this one?" The artist waved the painting to dry it.

"Yes, it's awesome!"

"You may have it." The painter turned it over. "What's your name?"

"Amanda."

He wrote something on the back and handed it to her. She read what he wrote.

Amanda –
Harmony on your horizons.
All blessings, Frank – Taos Pueblo

"Thanks so much, Frank." She dropped some coins into his tip jar. "This is amazing."

"Enjoy your visit to the *pueblo* tomorrow." Frank took out another piece of paper from a leather pouch and swirled his brush in a jar of water.

Amanda joined Caleb and the rest of the group. They continued to check out the town, returning to Mable Dodge Lohan's place in time for dinner. Cleo seemed much better but stuck close to Ms. Bowler.

"Did you have a nice time in town?" asked the teacher as she spooned guacamole on her enchiladas.

"You bet. We saw some cool sculptures and I met a native artist. He gave me one of his paintings!"

"That's very nice. You'll have to show it to me. Cleo and I spent some time in the library and found a copy of *The Laughing Horse*. It was fun to look through it and read what people thought was interesting a hundred years ago."

Cleo glanced up from her meal. "I forgot my meds in your room, Ms. Bowler. I'm supposed to take them with my dinner."

"I'll get them for you, sweetie." Ms. Bowler started to get up from the table.

"It's OK. I can get them myself."

"I'll come with you," said Amanda. She took the last bite of her spicy taco and followed Cleo.

Audrey met them at the door and handed them a large

flashlight. "This'll help you see better. It's getting dark out there. Watch for exposed tree roots on the pathway."

Amanda shone the light on the path, keeping an eye out for anything that could trip them. The girls arrived at the Gate House Cottage and collected Cleo's pills.

"What are those for?" asked Amanda.

"They're just for when I get anxious," replied Cleo. "Can I hold the flashlight on the way back?"

"Sure." Amanda handed it over.

Instead of pointing it down on the path, Cleo swung the light around, shining it on the trees and bushes. Amanda tripped and fell hard on the dirt path.

"Ouch!" She reached down to her left knee. Blood oozed through her jeans. "Oh, Cleo, shine that light over here. I think I cut myself or something."

Cleo let out a terrific scream, like from a horror movie. "Th-there's somebody in the bushes!"

8

AMANDA FELT A SHARP PAIN IN HER KNEE. "CLEO! STOP BEing such a drama queen and bring that flashlight here."

Cleo stood closer. The light from the flashlight illuminated her pale face. Her lips trembled.

"I saw a white face. It was a small man, maybe a dwarf."

"Could you please shine the light on my knee?"

Bright red blood seeped out of a rip in her jeans. Amanda tried to roll up her pant leg to have a better look, but her skinny jeans were too tight.

A rustle in the bushes followed by footsteps on gravel made Cleo gasp. "Maybe it's that guy I saw." She looked from side to side.

"Hey, what's going on?" Caleb materialized out of the darkness with a grin like a Cheshire cat. "What's taking you guys so long?" He noticed Amanda's leg. "Sheesh! What did you do now, Amanda?"

"I guess I tripped and fell on something sharp."

He looked at Cleo. "And what's with you?"

"Did you see anyone else? I think someone is hiding in the bushes. One minute he was there, the next he wasn't."

Caleb shook his head. "No, I didn't see anyone. Amanda, you better go get your knee checked out." He put his arm around Amanda and took the flashlight from Cleo. "I'll hold this to make sure nothing else happens to you two. Stick close, Cleo."

Cleo followed closely behind Caleb and Amanda. "I'm sure he's out there. In the bushes."

"Who are you talking about?" Caleb frowned.

"That little man I saw in the bushes. His face was bright white. He had an evil smile." Cleo shuddered.

Caleb shone the flashlight around. "See, look, there's nobody in the bushes." He swung it around once more to prove his point.

Cleo shrieked and grabbed his arm, knocking the flashlight to the ground and leaving them in darkness.

"I—I saw him. He was there again."

"Way to go, Cleo." Caleb picked up the flashlight and tried to turn it on, with no luck. "Now we have to make our way back in the dark."

Cleo began to sob.

Caleb hit the flashlight with the palm of his hand. It came back on and shone straight on a face peering out of the bushes.

The face of St. Francis.

Amanda snorted and shook her head. "If this is your little white man, you have nothing to be afraid of. That is not an evil smile, but the kindest smile I have ever seen on a statue. Now, let's get back before I'm totally soaked in blood." Her knee hurt and she had enough of Cleo and her drama.

That night Cleo went to bed early. "I'm sorry I made you angry." She pulled the covers up to her chin. "I hope your knee will be all right."

Amanda looked up from her tablet and smiled. "It'll be OK. I'm sorry I yelled at you. Now get some sleep."

Before she went to bed, Amanda wrote a funny little story on *Kidsblog* about phasmophobia and the face of St. Francis. 'At least Cleo is giving me lots of ideas for stories,' she thought as she drifted off to sleep.

💀 💀 💀

The next morning Ms. Bowler announced, "Today we're going to Taos Pueblo. This is an important historic site that dates back over a thousand years. It is considered to be the oldest continuously inhabited community in the USA. People still live there, so please respect their home. There will be many opportunities to take pictures and meet native artists. It's windy so make sure you wear a coat. Oh, and bring your swimsuits!"

The sun shone brightly again. Amanda couldn't understand why she would need a coat and a swimsuit but made sure she packed both. "Let's go, Cleo. The bus is waiting."

As they got on the bus, Caleb yelled from the back,

"Hey, have you seen any little white men lurking in the bushes, Cleo?"

The entire busload erupted with laughter. Cleo turned crimson. She slid into an empty seat and pulled her hood over her head, hiding her face.

"Cleo, why are ghosts such bad liars?" Caleb snickered. "Because you can see right through them."

Amanda shouted over the hooting and hollering, "All right, you guys. That's enough!" She dropped into the seat beside Cleo and squeezed her hand.

A few minutes later, the bus pulled up to a sign:

WELCOME TO **TAOS PUEBLO**
UNESCO WORLD HERITAGE SITE
THE RED WILLOW PEOPLE OF TAOS PUEBLO WELCOME
VISITORS AS THEY HAVE FOR OVER ONE THOUSAND YEARS

Amanda tingled with excitement as she viewed the village of adobe buildings arranged like building blocks. Snow-capped mountains loomed behind the *pueblo*. Solid terracotta houses, interrupted with splashes of bright blue doors, graced either side of a gentle creek. Simple wooden ladders leaned against the walls. Drying racks and clay ovens stood outside some of the houses. She couldn't wait to explore.

Ms. Bowler purchased tickets for everyone and then announced, "We have the entire morning here in the *pueblo*. You may recall that *pueblo* in Spanish means village. You are free to wander around and look inside any of the buildings with open doors. Be sure to chat with the artists, take notes and pictures. You might even find some items to buy as souvenirs. Do not go into the areas that say no entry. Some places are sacred and only the tribe members are permitted there. You are not allowed to climb on any of the structures or take pictures of the people or sacred sites without permission. We will all meet here at the entrance at noon. Enjoy yourselves."

Caleb put up his hand. "Can we take pictures of the houses?"

"Yes, as long as there are no people standing in front," Ms. Bowler cautioned.

Amanda saw a sign outside a building:

MORNING TALK INDIAN SHOP

She turned to Cleo. "This looks interesting, let's go in here."

Cleo hesitated. "Are you sure it's OK?"

A woman with a big smile appeared at the open door. "My name is Josita. Come on into my home and studio. I make all the pottery and jewellery here myself." She motioned with her hand. "I have a fire going to keep you warm."

The girls entered the warm, cozy dwelling, a welcome change from the chilly breeze outside. Walls held shelves of pottery. Tables displaying silver jewellery sat on colourful woven rugs. In one corner, a cheerful fire burnt in a round clay fireplace.

"Is there a special name for those round fireplaces?" asked Amanda.

"They are called kiva fireplaces," replied Josita.

"Kiva," Amanda repeated.

Amanda picked up a clay figure of a native woman with her mouth open. Small children perched on her knees, shoulders and all around her.

"How cute! I love this. Did you make it?"

"Yes, it is a storyteller. I make all my own storytellers as did my mother and grandmother before me. Clay storytellers represent the tradition of sharing stories with the future generations. Our language is not written down. It is only passed on through stories." Josita pointed to an assortment of figures. "If you look carefully, each one is different."

"I just have to buy one of these because I'm a storyteller too." Amanda studied the collection.

"Cleo, which one should I buy?" She glanced around the shop. "Cleo? Cleo, where are you?"

9

AMANDA PAID FOR THE STORYTELLER IN HER HAND AND LEFT the shop. She scanned the *pueblo* and spotted Cleo beside a clay oven, chatting to a man in a straw hat. When she got closer, she recognized Frank, the painter she met in town. Cleo munched on a cookie.

"Hello, Amanda." Frank held out a plate of pastries. "Would you like one? I just baked them in this centuries-old *horno*."

Amanda helped herself to a warm cookie and took a bite. "Mmmm. This is so good. Thanks."

"I live in the *pueblo*, over there." Frank nodded his head. "We share these outdoor ovens and bake our bread, cakes and pastries in them." Amanda noticed clay ovens scattered around the *pueblo* in front of many houses. "It looks like it did when the conquistadors first arrived, except for the doors. They have been added. At one time, ladders were the only way to get into the homes through openings in the flat rooftops. This was for safety. If an enemy approached, the ladders were pulled up and stored on the roofs. We don't have electricity or running water.

In this sacred village, we live as our ancestors did."

Amanda couldn't imagine not having electricity or running water. "Where do you get your water from?"

"Red Willow Creek." Frank pointed to a stream, lined with wispy willows, running through the middle of the *pueblo*. "Legend tells of an eagle that dropped two feathers, one on each side of the river, a sign for the ancient people to build the village at this spot."

"How many people live here?" asked Amanda.

"About one hundred and fifty, year round. More live here during the summer months. Make sure you get some fry bread from Maria and visit more artists. If you have any questions, I'll be around. Enjoy your visit." Frank nodded his head and walked away.

"This place is so cool!!" Amanda finished off her cookie and licked her fingers. "Where should we go next?"

"I think I'll just sit on that bench over there by the creek and do some sketching. It looks so peaceful with the willow trees bending over it."

"It sure does. I want to go into more of the shops, so I'll see you back here."

Amanda had a good time visiting with the artists in their homes. They made her feel so welcome. She approached an open blue door and stepped inside. A fire glowed in the kiva fireplace.

"Hello?" Amanda called.

No one answered.

"Hello! Is anyone here?"

She glanced around. Rustic hand woven baskets littered the floor and dream catchers hung on the whitewashed walls. Hand painted cards and colourful plates adorned a shelf. A small table stood in the entrance. On it sat a cozy-covered teapot, Styrofoam cups, and a note. Amanda picked it up and read it.

Stepped out for a few minutes.
Enjoy my art and help yourself to some warm tea.

'Wow, the person who lives here is sure trusting. What if someone came in and stole something?'

Amanda shivered. A gust of wind blew in. The door banged shut and the lights went out. The place became dark and scary. A creaking sound came from the roof. Amanda pulled the door but it wouldn't open. Something like a feather touched the back of her neck. She stood frozen.

Her breath, tight with fear, came in gasps. She had to get out—fast.

She remembered what Frank said about the rooftop entrances. She fumbled in the dark until she found the stairs. Clambering up them on all fours, she came to an opening in the ceiling. With one push, the glass cover opened onto the flat roof, empty except for a small potted cactus. Amanda's head whipped around to peer back down the stairs. She took a shallow breath. No one followed her and no one was on the roof. The top of a ladder poked up from the wall. She sprinted over to it, tripping over the cactus.

"Ouch!"

A sharp needle pricked her leg. She picked herself up and limped to the ladder. It didn't look very sturdy. Clinging to the rungs, she gingerly climbed down. At the bottom, she bumped hard into someone.

Amanda's hair stood up at the back of her neck. She hesitated, then turned around. That someone turned out to be Caleb.

"Amanda, wassup? You're not supposed to be climbing on the buildings, you know. Don't you just love this place! I got so many great pictures. How's your knee by the way? That was a nasty gash."

Amanda let out a breath and smiled. "It's fine. Doesn't hardly hurt anymore." Glad to see a friendly face, she steered him away from the scary house. "There are tons of things to take pictures of here."

"Where is your weird friend?" Caleb asked.

"If you mean Cleo, she's over by the creek, drawing. You shouldn't tease her, you know. She has issues."

"Like what?"

"Like she suffers from anxiety and stuff."

"Sorry, didn't know." Caleb shrugged. "I liked the story you wrote on *Kidblog*. I knew right away it was about her seeing that statue in the garden and thinking it was a ghost."

It must have been because of her story that Cleo got teased that morning. Amanda felt sick, she knew it was her fault.

Caleb stopped in front of a door with a sign:

FRY BREAD FOR SALE

"Let's get some fry bread." He pushed the door open. The smoky smell of hot oil greeted them. "Can we buy some fry bread, please?"

"Of course," said a woman with a long black braid over one shoulder.

The woman picked up a ball of dough and pressed it flat between her hands. She stretched it out with her fingers until it was as large and thin as a pizza shell and placed it in a pot of hot oil. The dough sputtered and crackled. When it turned a toasty brown, she removed it with tongs and placed it on a paper towel. The woman made the second one the same way, then placed the two pieces of fry bread on paper plates. "Careful," she said. "It's hot."

Amanda and Caleb sat outside at a table made out of an old barrel with a round piece of plywood on top. They poured honey over the warm bread.

"Yum, this is so good!" Amanda bit into the crisp, yet chewy bread.

Caleb nodded in agreement then stopped. "Wait. Don't take another bite."

"Why? What's wrong?"

"I need to take a picture."

"Well, hurry up."

After they finished, they wandered around, taking more pictures.

Caleb stepped behind a house and shouted, "Look at this, Amanda."

Amanda spotted a No Entry sign. "I don't think we're supposed to be here."

"I'll just take a couple of pictures."

Amanda's scalp prickled as she walked around the house to Caleb. He was aiming his camera at a circular enclosure made of poles. Two long poles stuck out from the middle.

"You're not supposed to be here." A large hand grabbed her shoulder. "Didn't you see the sign?"

Amanda flinched and turned around. Scowling at her was the man who had been so angry with them at the St. Francis church.

When he saw Caleb, his face turned lobster red. "And you, you are not allowed to take pictures. This is a sacred site." He reached for the camera.

Caleb pressed it close to his chest with both hands. "I'm sorry. I didn't know. We'll leave now."

The man grabbed the boy's arm. "You kids are nothing

but trouble."

"Leave the boy alone." Frank came up behind them. "They came in here by accident. It isn't a very big sign."

The man released his hold on Caleb and glared at Frank.

Frank ignored him and motioned to Amanda and Caleb. "You kids need to come with me, now. Your friend fell into the creek."

10

THEY RACED BACK TO THE CREEK. CLEO, SOAKING WET, shivering and sobbing, stood beside Ms. Bowler.

"What happened?" Amanda asked. "When I last saw you, you were sitting on the bench drawing."

"Sh—she pushed me," Cleo said through chattering teeth.

"What? Who pushed you?" Amanda looked around.

A woman brought a blanket and gently wrapped it around Cleo. "Bring her into my shop. I have a fire going and some hot chocolate."

"That's very kind of you," replied Ms. Bowler. "Thanks so much."

"Unbelievable!" Amanda looked at Frank. "Who would push her into the water?"

He shrugged. "Might have been one of the other kids playing a prank."

"Well, that'd be pretty mean." Amanda followed Cleo and the teacher into a shop scented with the sweet smell of soaps and lotions.

The owner of the shop, Estrellita, gave everyone hot

chocolate. Amanda noticed the colourful paintings on the wall depicting scenes from the *pueblo*.

"I just love your shop. Who did the paintings?"

"I did. The paintings, sculptures and pottery are all made by me. In my spare time, I make my own soaps and lotions." She handed Amanda a bar of soap that smelled like strawberries, mint and chocolate.

"You're a really talented artist."

"I am an artist, but my most important job is being a mother to my three children. My husband and I are raising them here in the *pueblo* so they will know their heritage firsthand."

"That is so cool." She sniffed the soap. "Mmm, this soap smells good enough to eat. I think I'll buy some for my mom. She'd love it." Talking to Estrellita made Amanda think of her mom and how she would enjoy visiting a shop like this.

She walked over to Cleo. "Are you warming up? You know the sign says to stay out of the creek since it's the residents' only source of drinking water."

Cleo managed a weak smile. "I was just drawing a picture of the creek when that girl came and pushed me in. I don't know why."

"What girl?"

"The girl in the white dress that's been following me around. You know, the one I drew at the hacienda." Cleo sighed. "I thought she liked me."

Amanda raised her eyebrows. Not sure what to say, she just patted Cleo's hand. "We don't have much time left and I still want to see the church and the graveyard."

"Go ahead. I'll be all right. I'm safe and warm here." Cleo took another sip of hot chocolate.

Amanda stepped outside. She looked around for Caleb, but he was nowhere to be seen. The wind got colder and stronger. She zipped up her jacket and pulled the hood over her head, glad she'd listened to Ms. Bowler's advice.

She took pictures of the San Geronimo church and then continued on to a ruin tucked behind houses. Crumbling gravestones and weathered wooden crosses were scattered around the remainder of a damaged brick bell tower. Among the weeds lay broken gravestones and crosses that had fallen over. Amanda felt a sudden sadness wash over her.

She pulled out her map and guide. It explained that the ruin was the original San Geronimo church, destroyed by the soldiers in retaliation for Governor Bent's murder. Only the battered bell tower remained standing. The graves belonged to the many who lost their lives in the fight.

The sun went behind a cloud. Tall grass leaped around the crosses as the wind whistled a mournful tune.

Amanda shuddered. A harsh breeze pushed her forward. Looking up at the sky, Amanda felt the wind push her again and she tripped over a rock. She stumbled hard into the low adobe brick wall surrounding the cemetery. Another shove sent her right over the fence. Her head hit a fallen brick. She saw stars before everything went black.

💀 💀 💀

She woke up, surrounded by crosses. Her head hurt. It took a few minutes to remember where she was. At first, she thought she had been dreaming. Amanda struggled to stand up. She held onto a cross. It fell over.

"Hey! You! What are you doing in there?"

An angry man waved his arms and shouted. He appeared all blurry. Amanda realized she was no longer wearing her glasses. She squinted and spotted them lying under another cross. She knelt down to pick them up.

"No point trying to hide, I can see you. Can't you read the signs? It says not to climb on any structures. It also says not to enter the graveyard."

Amanda stood up. When he got closer, she recognized the same angry man they had encountered earlier. She backed away.

"You! You are nothing but trouble!" Grabbing her by the arm, he pulled her out of the cemetery.

Amanda struggled to put on her glasses with one hand. "Ow, you're hurting me. Let me go!"

"Not until I take you to your teacher. I have had it with you kids poking your nose where you shouldn't." The man dragged Amanda back to Estrellita's shop.

Ms. Bowler looked up and gasped as they entered. "What is it? What's happened to you, Amanda?"

Amanda opened her mouth to speak, but the man bellowed, "This girl was in the graveyard, crawling around the crosses and causing damage. I caught her earlier at a sacred site with her buddy taking pictures!" His face turned scarlet and his nostrils flared like an angry bull. "This cannot be tolerated. These kids have no respect." He tightened his grip on her arm.

"Take it easy, Jim." Estrellita put her hand on his shoulder. "Let go of the girl."

The man released his hold. Amanda rubbed her arm and stared at the floor.

Ms. Bowler said, "I am so sorry." She pressed her lips tight and closed her eyes for a minute. "Come on everyone, I think it's time for us to leave." She frowned at Amanda and shook her head. "I am very disappointed in you, Amanda Ross. I expected you to be more respectful."

Amanda wanted to explain, but who would believe the wind blew her into the cemetery? Her head throbbed. If only a hole would open up in the floor and she could just disappear into it. With hunched shoulders and burning cheeks, she trailed behind the others, wishing she were anywhere but there.

11

AMANDA SAT ALONE, SLUMPED IN A CORNER OF A SEAT IN the back of the bus, fighting back tears. 'What's going on? Who pushed me into the graveyard? I didn't see anyone. Why are all these crazy things happening?' She sniffled. 'Now Ms. Bowler is mad at me.'

Amanda hated upsetting people; first Cleo and now her favourite teacher. She wished her travelling buddy, Leah, was with her. Sure, sometimes they got in a jam but at least they could rely on each other. For the first time ever on a holiday, she wished she was at home.

The bus stopped. Amanda had not been paying attention to where they were going. She looked out the window. They were parked in front of a large bridge crossing a deep ravine. Everyone got off the bus. Amanda didn't move.

Ms. Bowler approached her. "We are at the Rio Grande Gorge, Amanda. Come and have a look."

"No, thanks," Amanda mumbled and huddled closer into the corner. "I'll only get in trouble, again."

"Look, I don't know what happened at the *pueblo*. It's

so unlike you to get into trouble, but I don't want this to spoil the trip for you. Bring your camera and take a few pictures. You will want to write about this. Your story last night was excellent, by the way. I'm going to submit it to a writing contest—although we might change it up a little, you know, to protect the innocent." Ms. Bowler winked.

Amanda straightened up and smiled. "Really?"

"Come on, let's join the others." The teacher patted Amanda's hand.

They met Mr. Samson and the rest of the students by the bridge. "This gorge is two hundred and forty metres deep and eighty kilometres long," the teacher explained. "It is also the site of many ancient petroglyphs. There are supposed to be hidden ruins and hot springs at the bottom."

Amanda squinted as she peered down. The river at the bottom slithered through rocks and trees. The wind whipped her hair around and pushed at her back. Amanda gripped the railing. She didn't want to be pushed into the canyon the way she was shoved into the graveyard. It was a long way down. Her stomach quivered.

Mr. Samson pointed to the bridge. "Spanning the ravine is the Rio Grande Gorge Bridge which is the seventh highest bridge in the United States. It crosses the *Rio Grande*, which means Great River. For some unknown reason, there have been many suicides from this bridge. Studies are being conducted to see how these can be prevented."

A chill went through Amanda and she felt dizzy.

"You can walk along the bridge and take pictures if you wish," suggested Ms. Bowler. "Stay on the sidewalk. Remember, this is a highway."

Caleb ran ahead and stopped at a lookout. "Oh, man. This is fantastic!" He clicked away. "Amanda, get over here. You can get the best shots from this side."

Clenching the rail and fighting the wind, Amanda made her way to the viewpoint. The spectacular scene was like something on a TV travel show. She relaxed a bit and pulled out her camera to take some pictures, staying away from the railing.

Caleb hung over the rail to get a better shot.

"Don't fall!" Cleo screamed. "Someone fell from there recently."

Caleb moved back from the rail and shouted. "Chillax, why don't you, Cleo." He looked at Amanda. "What is with her? How did she know someone fell from here?" He touched his head. "Headcase, I tell you. Totally crazy."

"Maybe she is just concerned about you," Amanda countered.

"Ya, right. I think she's three tomatoes short of a salad if you ask me."

"OK, kids! Back on the bus," called out Mr. Samson.

Amanda sat with Cleo. "How did you know someone had fallen off the bridge from that spot?"

"I don't know, I just did. I could see the person topple over and fall to the bottom. It was awful." Cleo trembled. "They may have done it on purpose."

"You mean—they committed suicide?"

Amanda remembered how it felt like the wind pushed her into the graveyard. 'Maybe the suicides Mr. Samson mentioned were not all done on purpose.' She gave her head a shake. 'This is crazy. Why am I even thinking this way? I don't believe in ghosts or supernatural stuff. There has to be a logical explanation to all of this.'

Amanda needed to think of something else; this was all a bit much. "Where are we going now, Ms. Bowler?"

"It's a surprise. A very nice surprise," answered the teacher.

💀 💀 💀

The bus zigzagged through towering red cliffs and stopped at what looked like an oasis in the middle of nowhere. Palm trees waved in the breeze, flowering bushes coloured the gardens and large clay pots lined the gravel walkway. A bright sign stood outside.

WELCOME TO OJO CALIENTE

Ms. Bowler explained, "*Ojo Caliente* translated means "warm eye" but is more commonly known as "hot spring". Make sure you bring your backpacks with you. After we have lunch inside, we will be spending the afternoon here at the spa, enjoying the hot springs and swimming pool. Remember to speak softly. The hot springs and spa are designated a whisper zone in order to preserve the quiet and tranquillity."

With full stomachs, the students went through the gift shop and into the change rooms. They emerged clad in bathing suits. In front of them, two large pools waited. Along one side, water cascaded out of clay pots, falling into four hot pools dug out from the red cliffs. Signs indicated the cliff-side hot pools had different temperatures and ingredients.

Amanda couldn't decide which one to go in first. "Let's try this one." She dipped her toes in.

"Feels soooo good," said Amanda as she lowered herself into the warm, iron-rich water. "It's as relaxing as the sign said it would be."

Cleo followed. "Oh, this is nice." She closed her eyes and sighed.

After a few minutes, Amanda asked, "Where did you go to school before coming to Guy Weadick?"

Cleo kept her eyes closed. "I lived in Saskatchewan with my mom and stepdad. Things didn't work out so I moved to Calgary, to live with my dad and his girlfriend."

"What do you mean, 'things didn't work out?'"

"The kids at school were mean to me. That's when I started seeing things. My mom couldn't handle it. I spent some time in a hospital, which was awful. Then she sent me to live with my dad." Cleo's voice broke. "Mom said I was just doing it to get attention. She didn't believe the kids were cruel to me."

"You mean you were being bullied?"

"I guess so." Cleo looked down at her toes as she wiggled them in the warm water. "Thanks for sticking up for me when your boyfriend was picking on me this morning on the bus."

"You mean Caleb? He is *not* my boyfriend. He's a boy and he's my friend, but he is not my boyfriend." She slowly shook her head and then asked, "Why do you think you see ghosts anyway?"

"I don't know. They just seem to appear. I think the girl I keep seeing here wants to tell me something."

"You mean, you think she's a ghost?" She couldn't believe Cleo was being so calm about it, especially since she seemed to get so upset by ghosts. Amanda squeezed her eyes shut and opened them. "No, there must be a logical explanation."

Cleo looked up and covered her mouth to stop from screaming.

Someone, brown as a bear, stood above them with huge eyes and hands reaching out like a furious animal about to seize them.

12

"CALEB! WHAT ARE YOU DOING?" AMANDA PULLED A FACE. "Why are you all covered in mud?"

"You guys have just got to try this. It is so cool! You cover yourself in special mud and then after it's dry, you wash it off in a shower." He motioned with his hand. "Follow me."

Amanda sighed. "Come on, let's see what this is all about."

The girls got out of the hot pool and followed Caleb to another pool full of chocolate coloured mud. They covered themselves with the warm mud and lay in the sun while it dried. In the valley, the wind had disappeared and the sun felt warm as it baked the mud.

Amanda laughed. "You look so funny, Cleo."

"So do you!"

Amanda felt her skin tighten as the mud dried. After a few minutes, she stood under a shower and rinsed it away. "My skin feels so good," said Amanda as she dried herself with a rough towel.

She spotted Ms. Bowler. "Thanks for bringing us here.

I have never been to a spa before. I just love it."

"Glad you're enjoying yourselves."

"It is so peaceful here. I feel safe," said Cleo.

"I'm not surprised. These ancient springs have been a gathering place and source of healing for thousands of years. Warring tribesmen often set their weapons and differences aside to gather in peace at these springs. They enjoyed the benefits of the waters and healed their wounds together. Did you know that spa is an acronym for the Latin phrase, *salus per aquas*, which means health through water?"

"Really! That's awesome," exclaimed Amanda. "I thought acronyms were something modern."

"They've actually been around for a long time." The teacher chuckled. "If you get tired of the pools, there are some good hiking trails. There's an easy one to an old round barn not too far from here. Just don't take too long as it's getting late in the afternoon."

"That might be fun to check out. What do you think, Cleo? Do you feel like a short hike?"

"Sure."

"Can I come along with you guys?" asked Caleb.

"Of course, why not? The more the merrier." Amanda wrapped the towel around herself and headed to the change room.

Cleo scowled and followed.

Back in jeans and T-shirts, the three of them started

out. Amanda held the brochure and map she got from the front desk.

"It looks easy to get to. We just need to follow this trail and the signposts."

The area felt familiar to Amanda. The dry earth, sprinkled with sagebrush and odd-shaped rocks, reminded her of Alberta. In the distance, badlands lined the horizon. The late afternoon sun felt warm. Caleb and Cleo chatted as they walked along behind her. She took a deep breath, happy they were getting along. The horrible morning seemed like such a long time ago. Nothing could possibly go wrong now. Could it?

Small paths veered off the trail.

"Should we leave this trail at some point?" asked Cleo.

"I don't think so. According to the map, we should stay on this one. The smaller paths lead to the river and back to the gorge."

They came around a bend and saw a round building that looked like a giant toadstool.

"This is so cute." Amanda raced ahead and opened the door. The smell of old wood, varnish and hay greeted her. The kids went up the stairs and viewed openings where hay used to be pushed down to feed the cows below.

Amanda read from the brochure, "This barn is no longer used for dairy cows, but is let out for special occasions like weddings." She looked up. "This would be a totally awesome place to have a wedding, don't you think?"

"I wonder why it's round?" asked Cleo.

Amanda scanned the brochure. "It says it may have been designed round to keep evil spirits away."

Cleo trembled.

The door slammed shut.

"I h-have to get out of here." Cleo looked around for the stairs.

"Ya, let's go." Caleb found the stairs and started down.

He stopped halfway when a whistling sound echoed in the empty building. Cleo and Amanda looked at each other with wide eyes. "Come on, girls, follow me." Caleb continued down the stairs, the girls close behind him. He crossed the floor and pushed the door. It flung open with a bang as a gust of wind grabbed it.

Cleo dashed out like a greyhound and raced down the trail.

"Wait for us!" shouted Amanda as she helped Caleb close the heavy door.

They looked around. Cleo was nowhere to be seen.

"Cleo, where are you?" shouted Amanda as they headed down the path. Silence greeted her. "Now what?" She looked at Caleb.

He sighed and shook his head. "Oh brother. She must have gone down one of these side paths. But which one?"

The sun started to set. Bizarre shadows pranced ahead of them on the path.

"I think we should get back and let the teachers know

what happened," said Caleb.

"Maybe we should keep looking for her. I'm already in trouble and they will get mad at me for not keeping an eye on her."

"She's not your responsibility." Caleb shrugged. "Why would she run off like that anyway? One minute she seems normal and the next she is off her rocker. I just don't get it!"

Amanda examined the dirt beside her. "Let's look down this trail. I think I see foot prints."

"So, now you are a tracker?" Caleb punched her shoulder. "OK, just this one trail."

The weeds lining both sides of the path were almost as tall as them. Running water trickled in the distance. The light grew gloomy.

"I hope she didn't fall in the river." Amanda quickened her pace.

Twilight dimmed and then it turned black without warning, like it does in the desert. Amanda shuddered.

"Are you scared?" asked Caleb behind her.

"No, I am not!"

They heard rustling and then screeching.

A bird flew out of the weeds and circled above them.

Amanda grabbed Caleb's clammy hand. Her heart thundered.

The weeds parted.

Amanda squeezed her eyes shut.

13

WHEN AMANDA OPENED HER EYES, CLEO STOOD IN FRONT of her. She looked like a wild animal with her face covered in mud and her T-shirt dripping wet.

"Cleo!" Amanda let go of Caleb's hand and rushed to hug her. "What happened to you?"

"I had to get away from that barn. Bad things were in there. I could feel them. I ran down a path. I couldn't see that it ended at a sharp drop-off. I slid down a muddy bank and ended up at the edge of a river. It was so scary." Cleo shook from head to toe. "I finally dragged myself up the bank. I didn't know which path to take until I heard you guys calling me."

"We better get back," said Caleb. "Everyone will be wondering where we are."

They each took a hold of one of Cleo's hands and hurried down the trail. When they rounded a corner, they bumped straight into Mr. Samson.

"There you are!" His face turned a purply shade of red. "We are about to leave. Why can't you kids keep to the schedule?" He noticed Cleo. "And what happened to you, again?" He slowly shook his head as he led the way back.

It was pitch black when they drove back across the Rio Grande Bridge. Amanda felt Cleo shudder beside her. She squeezed her hand. There was obviously something terribly wrong with her. Amanda wished she knew how to help her.

☠ ☠ ☠

At breakfast the next morning, Ms. Bowler said, "I know we have some potters in the group so you will be pleased to hear we are stopping at a pottery studio on our way to Cimarron today."

"You sure planned some fun things for us to do on this trip." Amanda gulped down the rest of her chocolate milk. "The spa was amazing. I can't wait to tell my mom about it." Since the teacher was in a good mood, she decided not to bring up the *pueblo*.

"Well, I hope you're writing lots of notes and taking pictures. I expect some great articles and stories when we get back." Ms. Bowler winked at Amanda.

"I have some good drawings." Cleo held up her sketch pad.

"I tried doing pottery once," said Amanda. "My aunt has a pottery studio on a small island in British Columbia. When I visited her, she let me make a vase. It was a lot harder than it looked."

The bus drove out of town and into Taos Canyon. Bits of snow around the rocks and pine trees made Amanda glad she put on a warmer jacket.

They soon pulled into the driveway of a large house. Behind a mesh fence lining one side, freshly chopped wood stood piled high.

When she got off the bus, Amanda breathed in the fresh, clear air. "It smells like pinewood and cedar. I wonder what all that wood is for. They must have a fire-place."

A black cat ran behind a large clay pot near the balcony. The more Amanda surveyed the yard, the more pots she noticed.

She nodded her head. "This is a cool place."

Two women appeared on the deck above them. "Come on up. We've been expecting you."

Amanda headed the group as they climbed the stairs up to the front door. "OMG!" she said as they entered the house. "There is so much pottery! Did you make it all yourselves?"

"Welcome to Enchanted Circle Pottery. Most of the pottery here has been made by the couple who live here. They are away right now and we are looking after the place for them. We're potters too. There are a few pieces here made by us. I am Fran, by the way, and this is Dorothy." She pointed to the other woman. "Now, who here makes pottery or would like to?"

A number of students put up their hand, including Amanda and Cleo.

Fran led them through the house, pointing out pottery pieces and explaining the process. "You will notice the iridescent colours of the pottery. See how each piece has a different shade. This is because it has all been fired with wood. Wood firing, an ancient Japanese process, produces these unique tints. As the wood burns in the kiln at extremely high temperatures, the ash lands on the pieces and melts—forming a glaze. The flames licking the pots also add interesting marks. I'll show you the kiln later."

"Is that what all the wood is for?" asked Amanda.

"Yes, wood is cut and stored all year long. As much as five cords of wood are required for each firing."

"How hot does it get?" asked Caleb.

"It can get as high as 2400 degrees Fahrenheit," replied Fran.

"What is that in Celsius?" asked Amanda.

"I'm sorry, I forgot you use Celsius in Canada. Let me see." Fran thought for a minute. "It would be about 1300 degrees Celsius."

Amanda stood beside a pot as tall as her. Caleb snapped a picture.

"Man, that thing is huge." He grinned. "I wouldn't

want that to fall on me."

Every room held rows and rows of pots, including vases, bowls, jugs, goblets and mugs. A pair of horses and a graceful dove caught their attention. Amanda ran her hand over the rough and smooth textures of the dove. "I wish I was good enough to make something this amazing."

Fran took them outside to the enormous brick kiln. It was so big all ten of the students easily fit inside. The ceiling loomed high above them. Shelves for smaller pieces lined the walls.

"This is called a train style kiln. It holds a huge amount of pots and takes up to sixteen hours to load. During the forty hours of firing, the potters feed the wood into the kiln and rake the coals. They record the temperatures and make adjustments to ensure a successful firing. After one week of cooling, they open the door and unload the treasures."

Amanda thought about how hot it got in the kiln and started to sweat.

"Let's get out of here," she said to Cleo. "I feel claustrophobic."

Caleb stayed back to take more pictures while the rest of the group filed out the narrow door and back onto the driveway.

Amanda glanced up at the balcony and noticed a tall pot sitting on the edge begin to wobble. "Cleo, move!"

Amanda shouted as the urn toppled over.

Cleo seemed frozen to the ground. The vessel headed straight toward her.

Amanda grabbed her friend and pulled her out of the way, just as the pot smashed into a thousand pieces on the ground in the exact spot Cleo had been standing.

A black cat scampered down the stairs and into the woods.

14

No one said a word for a few minutes. Then Cleo, leaning on Amanda's shoulder, began to sob.

Ms. Bowler stared at the broken pieces of pottery scattered around the pavement. "Who would push that vase over?"

"No one could have pushed it. Everyone was here," replied Amanda as she patted Cleo's shoulder.

"Caleb isn't," said one of the other students.

"Where is he, anyway?" asked the teacher.

"I think he might still be inside the kiln." Amanda glanced over at the brick enclosure.

"The door is closed. I don't think anyone is in there." Fran tried the door to the kiln. "It's locked. That's weird. We never lock it when it isn't being used." She fumbled in her pocket, pulled out a key and opened the door.

A frazzled Caleb stumbled out. "That was so not funny, locking me in there!" The tips of his ears burned red. "Didn't you hear me knocking and calling?"

"The walls are so thick, you can't hear anything from outside," said Fran. "But, how did you get locked inside anyway?" She shook her head and sighed when she looked at the smashed pot on the driveway. "I'll go sweep this up." She glanced over at Cleo. "I'm so glad no one got hurt."

Ms. Bowler wrinkled her brow and mumbled, "Why do I get the feeling this trip is cursed?" Louder, she said, "Let's get on the bus, everybody."

💀 💀 💀

The bus took them further into the mountains. They passed tall pointy bluffs that looked like stone barricades protecting a meandering river below. Amanda grabbed her camera from her backpack.

"I have to take pictures of those awesome cliffs." She snapped pictures through the bus window. "I sure hope they turn out."

Ms. Bowler nodded her head. "They are called the Palisade Sills and were created when hot lava shot its way up through older rocks. They are quite unique to this area. Perhaps we can stop for better pictures on the way back."

Not long after, they arrived at a small frontier town called Cimarron. The bus stopped in front of the St. James Hotel, an old, two-story building painted beige with a white trim. The American stars and stripes flag flapped in the wind on top of the sign. Hitching posts ready for horses to be tied up lined the front.

Amanda's stomach rumbled. "Are we having lunch here?"

"Yes. We'll have lunch and then look around. You'll find this place interesting. Many famous people from the Wild West stayed here." Ms. Bowler led the way into the hotel.

The first thing Amanda noticed was the massive head of a bison hanging on one wall of the chandelier-lit lobby. Stag heads decorated other walls and a grandfather clock stood in a corner. The colonial furniture and western paintings, sculptures and cowboy artifacts gave the room a welcoming feeling. But, Amanda still felt uneasy.

"This is like stepping into a cowboy movie," said Caleb.

Amanda picked up a leather-bound guest book. Burnt into the cover, like a brand, were the words:

the St. James Hotel
Est. 1880

"This place has been around for a long time."

"We have reservations in the restaurant so we better get in there," Ms. Bowler announced as she walked toward a set of saloon doors.

Their table sat beside a fireplace under the massive head of a Texas Longhorn. The scary horns spanned the entire brick wall. Amanda wasn't sure if she was comfortable with the heads of animals around her, but put that thought out of her mind when she saw the menu.

"I'm going to have the bean burrito with green salsa. What are you having, Cleo?"

"It all looks good. It's so hard to decide. I love Tex-Mex food."

"I'm having a bison burger." Caleb smacked his lips.

A waitress with a huge smile arrived. "Hi, I'm Sadie. What can I get you kids to drink today?"

Once everyone placed their orders, Amanda asked, "How long have you worked here, Sadie?"

"Seven years," Sadie replied. "I love it here. But then, I'm not afraid of ghosts." She left to get the drinks.

Cleo paled. Amanda's mouth hung open.

Caleb flashed them a devilish smile. "Don't you know? This place is supposed to be haunted."

"How do you know that?" Cleo barely whispered.

"I did some research on the internet last night. There have been sightings of ghosts and paranormal activities here. Ghost Hunters International even filmed an episode here. After lunch, I plan to go ghost hunting myself. Do you want to come along, Cleo?"

Cleo bit her bottom lip and looked down.

"Leave her alone, Caleb." Amanda glared at him. "Maybe we should have left you in that kiln."

"Sorry, my bad." Caleb rolled his eyes and scratched his head.

Sadie arrived balancing a large tray of drinks. As she handed them around, Amanda asked, "Is there any proof there are ghosts in this hotel?"

"Well, I once set the table for a banquet in one of the large rooms. When I came back, the cutlery was all over the place. Another time I could smell roses in one of the hallways. There were no roses anywhere, in fact, it was wintertime. The late owner of the hotel wore rose scented perfume. My friend who works in the bar told me she saw a cowboy reflected in the large mirror behind the bar. When she turned around, he wasn't there." She shook her head. "These things may not be proof but it makes you wonder. Now, what do you all want to eat?"

Cleo swallowed. "I don't think I'm hungry anymore."

15

AFTER LUNCH, MR. SAMSON TOOK THEM INTO THE ADJOIN-
ing bar. A typical western saloon, it held a long counter
with bar stools along it, a huge ornate mirror and spit-
toons on the floor.

He pointed up. "Do you see those holes?"

Amanda noticed dark holes peppering the white tiled
ceiling.

"Those are bullet holes from gun fights. *Cimarron* is
a Spanish word meaning wild or unruly and this town
definitely lived up to its name. Many arguments were
settled by gunfights in the old days. Twenty-six people
ended their lives here in this very hotel."

"How horrible," murmured Amanda.

"Have a look around, take pictures and make notes,
but don't be a nuisance or get into any trouble." Mr.
Samson looked straight at Amanda and Cleo.

Amanda's cheeks reddened and she looked at Cleo.
"Let's get out of here." She didn't like being thought of
as a troublemaker.

They went back into the lobby and looked more closely at the artifacts on display. Amanda opened the guest book she had noticed earlier. On the first page, she read about famous people like Wyatt Earp, Annie Oakley and Buffalo Bill Cody. They once stayed at the hotel and their rooms were on display.

"Can we see the rooms upstairs?" Amanda asked the woman at the front desk.

"No, I'm sorry but there isn't a guide available today, and you are not allowed upstairs on your own. Overnight guests stay in the famous rooms."

Amanda pouted. "I really wanted to see these old rooms. We came all the way from Canada to see this."

Cleo tugged her sleeve and whispered, "It's OK. We don't need to see those scary old rooms anyway."

A man carrying a mop and a bucket came up behind them. "I can show you around if you'd like. I'm about to go up there anyway."

Amanda's eyes lit up. "Really! That would be so awesome."

"My name's Len. Just follow me," said the man. He unclipped the red rope, with a no admittance sign hanging from it, in front of the stairs.

"Hey, wait for me." Caleb arrived, breathless. "I like stuff about cowboys."

They followed Len up the creaking, ornate, carpeted stairs to a dimly lit stairwell. At the top of the stairs, a picture hung on the red and gold striped papered wall.

Cleo gasped when she saw the image of a young girl in white.

"It's just a picture, Cleo. There are no such things as ghosts." Amanda pursed her lips.

Len replied, "Some say there are ghosts in this hotel and others say it's hogwash." He chuckled. "I guess you can believe whatever you want."

The man flicked on a switch lighting a narrow hallway. Tilted chandeliers illuminated closed doors along each side. On each door hung a sign.

Amanda walked up to the first door and read out loud. "Room 21 William J. Cody."

"That's the real name of Buffalo Bill Cody," said Caleb.

"Yup, it sure was and he slept in this very room," said Len.

Caleb read the next sign, "Room 22 Zane Grey. Hey, he wrote cowboy stories that my grandpa lent me to read."

"Look over here, this is the room Annie Oakley slept in. She had an exciting life. I did a book report on a biography of her. Can we look in some of these rooms?" asked Amanda.

"Sure, I have keys for some of the ones that are not currently being let out. We can visit the room Wyatt Earp stayed in. Do you know who he was?"

"I do," said Caleb. "He was a sheriff and he and his brothers had a shootout with some outlaws at the OK Corral in Tombstone, Arizona. My parents and I went on a holiday there. We watched a pretend gunfight. It was way cool."

"Wyatt Earp and his brothers stayed in this hotel on the way to Tombstone." Len pulled out a huge bundle of old fashioned keys.

"Ouch. Stop that." Cleo shook her head.

"What's wrong?" asked Amanda.

Cleo clasped the back of her neck and glared at Caleb. "Someone pulled my hair."

"Don't look at me. Maybe the ghost of Annie Oakley pulled your hair." Caleb teased.

Amanda gave him a stern look. "A hair probably got caught in your hoodie. It happens to me sometimes. Come on, let's look in Wyatt Earp's room."

Len showed them a few of the famous rooms and explained how they had been restored to look exactly like they did in the 1800s. Amanda liked the old beds with puffy down quilts and brass headboards. Decorated water jugs and bowls sat on ornate dressers. Each room had a cozy fireplace. Amanda kept feeling like someone was watching her as she went from room to room. She noticed Cleo looking over her shoulder too.

"If you smell roses in this next room, it may be Mary Lambert. She always wore rose-scented perfume."

"Was she the owner of the hotel?" asked Amanda.

"Yes, Mary was the wife of Henri Lambert, the man who built the St. James Hotel. Together they operated the hotel and raised five children. She was a hardworking woman and well respected in the community. They say she still watches over the hotel and protects the people in it."

"This room is pretty." Amanda sniffed but couldn't smell roses. She murmured to Caleb, "They probably just spray rose scent around, to fool everyone."

When they were almost at the end of the hallway, Len stopped and turned around. "This is as far as we go, kids. We are not allowed to go into Room 18."

"Why not?" asked Caleb.

"That is the cowboy, T. J. Wright's room. One night in 1881, after winning at the gambling table, he was shot from behind as he left the gambling room. He crawled to his room and bled to death. But it seems his angry spirit never left. Many folks say they've seen him wandering around the hotel at night."

Amanda felt a chill go through her when she glanced at the padlocked room.

Ring Ring!

The maintenance man reached into his pocket and pulled out a cell phone.

"Yup, I'll be right there." Len put the phone back in his pocket. "I have to go. A problem with one of the toilets. Come on, kids."

16

CALEB AND CLEO FOLLOWED LEN DOWN THE HALLWAY. Amanda stood riveted to the spot. A shrill whistle filled the air. An icy cold shiver ran through her body.

Creak...

Amanda's shoulders tightened. She stared at the padlocked door to Room 18. It had opened a crack.

The hair on her arms lifted. Her breath came in rasps.

She sensed someone in the hallway. Her scalp prickled. She wanted to run, to scream, but she was petrified. With a clammy hand, she reached for the handle of the door to Room 19 beside her. The knob turned and the door opened.

Slipping inside, she leaned against the door to make sure it stayed shut tight. Her belly ached as if it had been kicked and the air was knocked out of her. Wiping the beads of sweat from her upper lip, she peered through the dim light. The room looked similar to the others they had visited.

Something scratched at the door. Panic welled up inside her. Wide-eyed, Amanda ran to the bed. Lifting the patchwork duvet, she climbed under the covers and pulled them over her shaking head. Heartbeats thundered in her ears.

Someone was in the room.

Even under the down quilt, her entire body shivered from the cold. Something touched the comforter. Her muscles froze. Scuffling sounds neared the bed.

A latch clicked. A window opened.

Everything went silent. Amanda waited for a few minutes, then slowly uncovered her head and glanced around. A faint scent of roses surrounded her. The room became brighter and warmer. The sheer curtains fluttered in the open window. She no longer felt afraid.

Amanda got out from under the covers and smoothed the bedding. She tiptoed to the door and gradually opened it. She peered down the hall. Nothing.

Without looking at Room 18, T.J. Wright's room, she dashed to the stairs and ran down them as fast as she could.

Once in the lobby, she took a deep breath and looked for her friends. No one was around, not even the woman behind the reception desk.

"Where is everyone?"

Amanda walked through the swinging doors into the restaurant. No one was there either. She went out a back door to the outside eating area and surveyed the empty tables and chairs. She stopped to listen. It felt like something was beside her. As she slowly turned to look, a huge bear leaned out a window holding a pie.

She opened her mouth to scream. Her throat seized up and nothing came out.

"What's wrong with you, Amanda?" Cleo appeared from around a corner. "You look like you just had a run-in with a ghost. Oh, that's right, you don't believe they exist."

Amanda gave her head a shake. The window with the bear holding the pie was just a mural painted on the wall.

She laughed nervously. "For a minute I actually thought that bear was real. That's a good painting."

Cleo shrugged her shoulders up to her ears. "You thought the bear was real, but you don't believe me when I tell you I see ghosts?"

"Where is everyone, anyway?" asked Amanda.

"They're in the gambling room, listening to stories about the guys that have been shot here in this hotel. The boys think it's cool but I think it's depressing."

"Did they talk about T. J. Wright, the cowboy from Room 18?"

"Oh, yes. Apparently, he harasses guests here all the time. But the ghost of Mary Lambert, who is called the protector, often chases him away. She doesn't like her guests being upset. He sometimes goes into the room next to his and bothers whoever is in there. Room 19, I think it is. It used to be the room of Mary Lambert's daughter."

"Really?" Amanda paled. She remembered the rose scent in Room 19 and wondered if Mary Lambert had chased T.J. Wright away. That is if it was him, or rather his ghost, in the room with her. Amanda flapped her hand. "No way! I don't think so. It's probably just a publicity stunt to increase business for the hotel."

"Whatever," mumbled Cleo.

The courtyard filled up with the other students.

"There've been some cool shootouts here." Caleb walked over to the girls. "Have you two been ghost hunting? This would be the perfect place." He glanced at Amanda. "You look a bit pale. You OK?"

"I'm all right. Just feel a bit funny, that's all." Amanda looked away.

Cleo laughed. "She thought the bear painting was real."

"No way!" Caleb chuckled. "It is a good painting, mind you." He pulled out his camera and took a picture. "I got some great shots today. Can't wait to download them. I even got a picture of the place T.J. Wright was shot."

Amanda swallowed and shoved her hands in the pockets of her jacket.

Her face lit up when Ms. Bowler appeared and said, "If you have seen and heard enough, we should get back."

"That's a great idea. I think we've all heard enough about people being shot and ghosts running around." Amanda headed for the bus.

Cleo slid in beside her. "That place was full of ghosts, but most of them were harmless. The girl that's been following me wasn't there, though." Cleo sighed and pulled out her sketch pad.

After a few minutes, Amanda looked over Cleo's shoulder and saw a young cowboy. Sad eyes stared back at her from the page. A shiver cut through her like the blade of a knife. Amanda leaned back in her seat and closed her eyes. Confused, she tried not to think of her weird experience at the hotel. But, she had a nagging feeling something about it seemed familiar.

Then she remembered: that bad dream. The nightmare she had back home when they were planning the trip to New Mexico. The one where she woke up under the covers and couldn't breathe. The one where she dreamt there was a ghost in the room with her.

17

By the time the bus brought the students back to Taos, it was already dark with a storm brewing. Lightning scarred the sky and thunder echoed across the mountains. The wind howled like a werewolf. Amanda zippered up her jacket before leaving the bus.

Everyone was glad to be inside. After dinner, the exhausted students retired to their rooms. Cleo didn't say much. She drew in her sketchbook. Amanda sent a quick email to her parents. Then she started a long one to Leah. She just had to tell someone about what happened at the St. James Hotel. Instead of sending it, though, she put it into a draft folder. Leah might think she had lost her mind. Maybe she had.

Amanda got bored, so decided to go to the library to find something to read. She skimmed the books, many by writers who had stayed in the Mable Dodge Lohan house over the years. Her eyes landed on a tattered copy of *The Laughing Horse* magazine. She picked it up and started to look through it when Caleb came in.

"Hi!"

"Oh, hi." Amanda looked up from the magazine. "What're you doing here? You looking for something to read too?"

"No. Actually, I was looking for you. I need to show you something."

"Like what?"

"Well, I downloaded the pictures I took today and the ones from the gambling room are kind of odd. Do you want to come to my room and see what I mean?"

"OK, sure." Amanda put the magazine down on the coffee table in the middle of the room and followed Caleb.

"Welcome to the Ansel Adams Room." Caleb opened the door to the room he shared with another boy.

"Wasn't he a famous photographer?"

"Yes, he was. One of the best." Caleb was already at his computer screen. He showed Amanda the pictures he took that day.

"You sure got some great shots." Amanda could see why they had put Caleb in this room.

"Thanks, but take a look at this."

Amanda peered at a dark picture of the gambling room. A round card table covered with a white table-cloth stood in the middle. Wooden chairs were arranged around it. Above one chair, a round light glowed like a translucent snowball.

Amanda tipped her head to one side. "There could just be something wrong with your camera."

"It's weird. Doesn't matter what angle the picture is taken from, that same light is in every picture of that room."

Caleb clicked through five more shots showing the light above the chair. "It's not in any shots of other areas of the hotel." He showed her photos of the bedrooms, dining room and bar. "What do you make of that? This was the room where T.J. Wright was supposed to have been shot." Caleb's voice had risen an octave.

"I'm sure there is a reasonable explanation," said Amanda. But she wasn't so sure anymore. "I better get back to the library. I want to get that magazine and read it in my room."

"Would you like me to come with you?"

"Thanks, but I'll be OK." Amanda grinned. She was grateful for his concern, but she could look after herself.

Walking through the dark, quiet lounge, she entered the library. The magazine wasn't on the coffee table where she left it. She looked around the room and spotted it on a couch, open.

'Hmm, someone else must have been reading it. I wonder who?'

She picked it up and started to walk out of the room when a flash of white appeared in the corner of her eye. Amanda stopped and looked to the side. There was nothing. The flash appeared again as she entered the lounge. She stopped. Her heart quickened. "This is ridiculous.

There's nothing here," she whispered.

She took a step, then stopped abruptly. In front of her stood a young girl in a white flowing dress with her hands over her face.

Amanda gasped, closed her eyes and mumbled, "I don't believe in ghosts. I don't believe in ghosts. There is no such thing as ghosts."

When she opened her eyes, the image was gone. Not looking left or right, she ran back to her room.

Cleo looked up from her drawing. "You saw her, didn't you?"

"Wh—what do you mean?" Amanda quivered.

"I can tell that you saw the girl. The one I've seen. I think she wants to tell us something."

Amanda laid on her bed. "I didn't see anything." Her heart raced. She took a few deep breaths to calm down.

She opened the magazine and flipped through the yellowed pages. Cartoons of ghosts floating over people in their beds and articles about paranormal activity in Taos caught her attention.

'Really? I can't get away from this stuff. No wonder my eyes are playing tricks on me.' She turned a page. A folded piece of newspaper floated to the floor.

She picked it up, unfolded it and started to read. "Listen to this, Cleo. This article says that a letter written by a teenage girl to herself arrived twelve years after she died. How weird is that?"

"Let me see." Cleo took the article from Amanda's hand and skimmed it. "It says here her parents, Jim and Alma Jaurez, knew nothing about the letter and were shocked when it arrived at Alma's mother's place. The young girl wrote about her life, her family and her future. She wrote how thankful she was for everything her parents had given her and that she loved them very much. It doesn't say how she died. No one seems to know who mailed it and why it was sent to her grandmother's address." Cleo looked up from the article. "Incredible!"

"Jim Jaurez?" asked Amanda. She wondered if that was the same angry Jim they encountered at the *pueblo* and the church yard.

"Yeah, that's what it says." Cleo's face glowed with excitement.

Amanda rubbed her eyes. "This day is just getting weirder by the minute. Maybe we should just go to sleep. Tomorrow is our last full day here. I really hope it doesn't involve ghosts or messages from the dead. I am so done with all of this." She looked around. "Now where is that magazine? I thought I left it on my bed!"

18

"ARE WE GOING SOMEPLACE ON THE BUS AGAIN TODAY?"
Blueberry juice ran down Caleb's chin as he stuffed pancakes in his mouth.

"Caleb, don't talk with your mouth full." Ms. Bowler puckered her brow. "No. Today we're going to the Kit Carsen Museum. We can walk to it from here."

"I don't like museums," another student said.

"This one is very interesting. It's the house Kit Carsen lived in with his family. You will learn all about Taos' most famous frontier man in the 1850s. Another chance for great photo ops, drawings and story ideas." She turned to Amanda. "I'm surprised you didn't write anything about the St. James Hotel on *Kidblog*."

"I wrote something but just didn't post it yet." Amanda looked away and thought, 'No one would believe what I wrote anyway.'

💀 💀 💀

When they arrived at the museum on Kit Carsen Road, the students collected around Ms. Bowler in the courtyard.

"Who has heard of Kit Carsen?"

Caleb's hand shot up. "I have. He was a mountain man and gunfighter. My grandpa has a book about him."

"You seem to be the resident authority on cowboys and the Wild West, Caleb. You're right, but he was much more than that, as you will see. Among other things, he was a devoted husband and father. This house is where he lived for twenty-five years with his wife, Josefa, their eight children and several Indian children they adopted."

"Why did you call them Indian children? Shouldn't it be, First Nations children?" asked Amanda.

"In Canada, we now call the indigenous people First Nations, and in the United States, they are called Native Americans. In the 1800s, the time of Kit Carsen, they were called Indians," replied the teacher.

"This is the courtyard where much of the daily family activity took place. Inside the home, you will notice the rooms are sparsely furnished. They are exactly like when the Carsen family lived here. Fireplaces heated each room. The floors would have been dirt mixed with ox blood and wood ash to keep them hard and dust free. In one room, there is a video about Kit Carsen's life. Take notes and pictures. There may be a test later." Ms. Bowler laughed. "Just joking."

The students entered the simple one-story adobe building through the long porch at the front. Amanda

97

and Cleo worked their way through the kitchen, bedroom and children's room. Pictures of the family hung on the walls alongside articles about them.

Cleo stopped in front of a picture of a beautiful young woman holding a baby. "Who is this?" she asked.

"Let's see." Amanda read the plaque beneath the picture out loud, "Josefa Jaramillo, the third wife of Kit Carsen, was the beautiful fourteen-year-old daughter of a prominent Taos family. She was a tough, hardworking woman who almost singlehandedly raised their seven children and three adopted children while Kit was away during the war. Josefa and her sister, the wife of New Mexico Governor, Charles Bent, were in the Bent home when the Governor was attacked and killed. They escaped by scraping a hole in the wall."

Amanda looked up. "I remember this. We learned about that attack when we went to the Bent Museum." She returned to the article.

"She died in 1868 after giving birth to their eighth child, Josephine. Kit Carsen was so broken-hearted he died less than a month later."

Cleo gulped. "That poor baby never knew her parents. I wonder what happened to little Josephine."

Amanda looked closely at the picture. "To think Josefa got married when she was only fourteen. She was only two years older than us!" Amanda cringed.

Just then Caleb burst through the door. "You guys need

to come and watch this video. It's just in the next room. Did you know Kit Carsen was illiterate? Like he couldn't read or write, but he could speak English, Spanish, French and a whole bunch of Native languages. Amazing! He accomplished so much and had no education. He couldn't even sign his own name until he was older."

"OK. OK. We'll come."

The girls followed the eager Caleb into what would have been the office. The video explained how Kit Carsen was a mountain man, explorer, scout, trapper, cattle and sheep rancher, officer in the US Army, transcontinental courier, and US Indian Agent. He became a mythical folk hero to many Americans.

Amanda was finding the video interesting when it stopped abruptly and the lights went out. Cleo clutched her arm. A girl emerged from the darkness, her tattered white dress fluttering. Her hands covered her face. She floated above the floor and disappeared into the shadows.

Seconds later, the lights came on and the video continued.

"Did—did you see that?" Amanda looked at Caleb.

"Did I see what? I couldn't see anything. It was pitch black. Probably just a power outage."

Cleo stared at the wall and quivered.

"Don't tell me you're seeing things now too, Amanda." Caleb tilted his head to one side and frowned.

"Of course not," she scoffed. "Let's go into the gift

shop."

As they entered the shop, Amanda noticed a man leaving. She thought it was Jim, the man who had been so angry at the church and later at the *pueblo*. He left before she got a better look.

The hair lifted on the back of her neck.

Why was he always around when strange things happened?

19

"CAN WE SEE SOME BOOKS ABOUT KIT CARSEN?" ASKED Amanda.

The woman in the gift shop smiled and pointed to a bookrack. "There are some good ones over there."

Caleb picked up a book. "Hey, this is the one my grandpa gave me to read."

"There were lots of other books written with him as a hero but they are just fictitious adventures. He was America's first western hero. It is said Mr. Carsen was embarrassed by it all," explained the woman. "In everyone's eyes he was a huge man but in real life, he was only five foot six. His wife, Josefa, was actually a bit taller than him."

"I was wondering, what happened to the children after both parents died, especially the baby, Josephine?" asked Cleo.

"From what I understand, the five younger children were raised by Kit Carsen's brother-in-law, Thomas Boggs, and his wife."

Cleo leaned over and whispered in Amanda's ear, "I

wonder if it was the ghost of Josephine we just saw."

Amanda pursed her lips and shook her head.

"Let's go. I'm hangry!" said Caleb.

"Uh, 'hangry?'" asked Cleo.

"I'm so hungry it's making me angry." Caleb rubbed his stomach.

Ms. Bowler entered the shop. "I heard that. If you are finished looking around, we can all go to Doc Martin's for lunch."

"That's so funny." Amanda giggled. "My dad wears Doc Martens. Why would they name a restaurant after shoes?"

"It's not named after the boots, Amanda. They're actually spelled differently. This is a restaurant located in the former home of Doctor Thomas Paul Martin, the first, and only doctor in Taos for a long time."

After a delicious lunch, the students walked around the town square, stopping in the shops surrounding it. A band played in the centre under the American flag flapping in the breeze.

Ms. Bowler pointed to the flag. "Did you know in Taos that flag flies 24-7? Not many places are allowed to fly the flag continually. It is allowed at this spot because Kit Carsen and three other men guarded it for four days and four nights to protect it during the American Civil War." The teacher glanced at her watch. "We better get back so you can get your costumes ready for the Halloween party tonight. Come to my cabin if you want your face painted."

☠ ☠ ☠

Amanda entered the dining room and was greeted by a cowboy. A black hat hung low over his face.

"Caleb, is that you?" she asked.

The cowboy lifted his hat revealing an evil skeleton face. "I'm T.J. Wright, here to avenge my untimely death." His mouth twisted as it produced a menacing laugh.

Other students appeared in Day of the Dead costumes. A skeleton wearing a doctor's smock joined them. "Cool costume, Amanda. You're the best dressed skeleton here. Great job on the painted skull face. Who are you?" asked the voice of a classmate.

"I'm La Catrina." She smoothed her fancy dress and ran her hand up the large feather sprouting from an oversized hat. "I read about the elegant skeleton in the *Laughing Horse* magazine. Who are you?"

"I'm Doc Martin. Would you like me to check your heartbeat?" The skeleton held up his stethoscope. "Or do you have one?"

"Where is your weirdo friend?" asked the dead cowboy.

"If you mean Cleo, she'll be along soon. She wasn't ready yet."

Boom! Thunder crashed. The lights went out.

Audrey came in the room and quickly lit candles,

giving the room an eerie glow. White skeleton faces of the students bobbed in the air looking like disembodied heads.

The kids gasped as a girl with a pale face and flowing white dress rose from a well of darkness. The apparition hovered in the doorway then slowly drifted into the room.

Amanda's heart quickened. 'Was this the girl I saw last night?'

The girl looked straight at her and smirked. "Do I look like a ghost, Amanda?"

A tall, white haired *Doña Sebastiana*, in a black dress painted with a white skeleton, emerged beside the girl. "You children must behave, or I will take you away." She waved her long finger.

The lights came back on. "That's a good costume, Cleo. I think you had everyone believing you were truly a ghost." Ms. Bowler lifted her *Doña Sebastiana* skeleton mask. "We're ready for our ghost walk, so meet me at the front door in ten minutes."

"That should be fun. Don't you think?" Caleb shoved his toy pistols into their holsters. "Hey, Amanda, why are skeletons so calm?" He paused a minute and chuckled. "Because nothing gets under their skin."

"Ha ha! You think you're such a funny guy, Caleb." Amanda headed toward the door.

She wasn't sure about going on a ghost walk but decided it would be fine since she didn't really believe in ghosts anyway. Besides, it might be fun.

☠ ☠ ☠

A full moon shone between the branches of an old tree in front of the Governor Bent Museum where Ms. Bowler and the kids met a guide for the ghost walk. The air felt heavy with mist. Shadows from streetlights sprang in front of them. A yowling cat broke the silence.

Cleo hung onto Amanda's hand with a tight grip as they followed the guide. They listened with wide eyes to her stories of ghost encounters around town. It seemed like Taos was a haven for ghosts.

The group rounded a corner. Through the mist, a girl stood in a delicate white dress. She pointed to Cleo and opened her mouth as if to say something. Cleo screamed. The apparition vanished.

"Cool trick," said Caleb as he continued down the street. He stopped suddenly and bounced back. "What's this? Looks like someone strung a rope across the path. In this dark and mist, I didn't see it."

The guide examined the barrier. "Now that's odd. Who would do that?" She led the group to the town square and waited under the flag until all the children gathered around her. "This is where the people who murdered Governor Bent were hung. Some say their spirits haunt this place at night."

Amanda shivered. Maybe going on a ghost walk wasn't

such a good idea.

Bang!

The streetlights went out. The kids huddled together in the dark. A few minutes later the lights came on. Ms. Bowler and the guide had disappeared.

"Now what do we do?" Amanda asked as she peered into the distance.

Cleo whimpered and grabbed onto Amanda. "Where could they have gone?"

"Don't worry. We can find our way back to our rooms," said Caleb in a somewhat shaky voice.

Caleb led them down a dirt road past some creepy old houses. The students kept close together, Amanda on the heels of Caleb. No one said a word.

Suddenly, the door of one house flew open. A tall man emerged from the shadows.

"Get away from here! Stop coming around where you're not wanted," he hollered.

The kids changed direction and sprinted down the road. Heavy footsteps thumped closer and closer behind Amanda. She stopped abruptly, bumping shoulders with Caleb. Someone had grabbed the back of her collar. She noticed Caleb was also in his grip.

"You can't fool me with your costumes. I know who you are." The foul smell of alcohol wafted over their heads.

Even in the dark, she knew who the man was. Amanda

squirmed until she got loose from his hold. She spun around and looked straight into Jim's bloodshot eyes. "What—is—your—problem?"

Jim let go of Caleb. He grasped Amanda's shoulders. His eyes softened. "Tomorrow is *Dia de los Muetros,* The Day of the Dead. Come to the graveyard." Shoulders slumped, Jim turned and walked back to the house.

Amanda heard Ms. Bowler calling them and then saw her across the street.

"We're over here," Cleo shouted.

"Oh, thank heaven." Ms. Bowler let out a big breath. "We've been frantic. We went to investigate what happened and when we came back a minute later you were gone. How many times have I told you to stay in one place? Amanda, I thought you would know better."

💀 💀 💀

Later that evening, Caleb found Amanda sobbing in a corner of the garden.

"There you are. I've been looking all over for you. What's wrong?"

"This trip has been a disaster. I don't know what to think anymore. I don't believe in ghosts, but something pushed me into the graveyard at the *pueblo.* There sure seemed to be one in that hotel in Cimarron and last night I thought I saw one here in this house. And I keep getting into trouble. It's as if a ghost is causing it."

"That's just plain crazy and you know it. Cleo must be rubbing off on you." Caleb held out his hand. "Besides, it was my fault we left the square tonight, not yours or a ghost's. Come inside. You don't want to ruin your cool costume. They're serving hot chocolate in the dining room."

Amanda wiped tears off her face, smudging her make-up. "Oh no! Now I look a mess."

"Not any worse than usual." Caleb laughed as he grabbed her hand and pulled her along into the house.

20

THE NEXT MORNING AMANDA APPROACHED MS. BOWLER.
"Today is the Day of the Dead. It's when people here go
to visit the graves of loved ones. I've done some research
and it sounds interesting. Can we go to the cemetery to
see this?"

"That's a good idea. We have nothing planned for this
morning."

On the way to the cemetery, Ms. Bowler explained
some of the history. "The Day of the Dead is an old
Mexican tradition. It's a time of celebration and remem-
brance. Families visit the gravesite to clean and decorate
the graves of loved ones. Often candles, flowers and the
favourite foods of the deceased are placed on the grave.
The family eats, sings and tells stories about those who
have passed away. Participation by the children is important as they dance with cartoon figures of death, eat
skull sugar candies and learn not to fear death. They
learn to enjoy and appreciate every moment of life." She
caught Cleo's eye and smiled.

Once there, Amanda noticed many people going into

the opened gates carrying flowers, fruits, candies and even stuffed animals. She joined her classmates as they followed the crowd through the entrance.

Amanda teared up when she saw people placing items on graves. But she observed they were cheerful as they tidied the area around headstones and lovingly arranged flowers.

Then she noticed Jim. He placed a china doll by a small gravestone. She walked over and read the inscription.

Sonia Juarez, age 12

Loving Daughter of James and Alma Juarez

Amanda gulped. "Is this your daughter?"

"Yes," said Jim. "She was only twelve years old when she died of leukemia." A tear slipped down the big man's cheek. "When I see other children laughing and enjoying life, I get so angry. I get even more annoyed when I think they are making fun of our old way of life." He heaved a sigh. "My wife couldn't handle my anger and left me many years ago. I only wish I could hold my daughter one more time and tell her that I love her." Jim looked away to hide his tears.

Amanda noticed Jim's shoulders shaking. "I'm sure your daughter knows how much you love her." She placed her small hand over his large one.

Glancing at the date on the headstone, she realized

Sonia died fifteen years ago.

"Was it your daughter who sent a letter to herself which didn't arrive until recently?"

"I believe so, but I haven't seen the letter." Jim's chin trembled.

"I just read about it. The article said she wrote about her good life and her wonderful parents. She wouldn't want you to be angry, Mr. Juarez."

The big man turned around and smiled through his tears. He gave her hand a gentle squeeze.

"Also, we have not been making fun of your old ways. We find it all very fascinating. I plan to write a story about it when I get back home."

"I'm sorry for being so mean to you kids." Jim's voice cracked. "Thanks for coming to honour my daughter's grave. She would have liked you."

As they walked out of the cemetery together Amanda asked, "Why are there bones in the old house by the church?"

"We were planning to pull those old houses down when we discovered a human bone. So we started digging under the house and found more. We are still trying to figure out who they belong to and why they're there. It's all hush-hush. No one knows about them yet. So maybe don't put that in your story." He winked.

Cleo ran up to Amanda all out of breath, eyes shining. "She's here. I know she is here in this cemetery!"

"Who?"

"The girl, I mean the ghost of the girl I've been seeing. You know, the one at the *hacienda* and at the *pueblo*. I figured out what she's been trying to tell me. She wants me to know that a long time ago she was bullied and couldn't handle it. So she jumped off the bridge. She doesn't want me to do something like that." Cleo looked like a huge weight had been lifted from her shoulders.

"Did she tell you this?"

"No, not really. But I just know that's what she's been trying to tell me." Cleo sighed as she looked up to the clear blue sky.

Amanda suddenly understood just how important it was for Cleo to believe she had seen this ghost and that the ghost had a message for her. She reached for her and gave her a huge hug.

💀 💀 💀

Jim came to the Mabel Dodge Lohan house to see the students off later that afternoon. He apologized for his actions and welcomed the children back anytime.

Amanda was pleased to see a smile on his rugged face. "It was nice to meet you, Jim. Good luck with your investigations. Perhaps you can let me know what you find."

The big man bent down and gave Amanda a hug. "Thanks," he mumbled as he pressed a small object in her hand. "Good luck with your writing."

She unclasped her hand and found a small silver *milagro* of a hand holding a pen.

"Thank you so much. I will treasure this forever." Amanda grinned from ear to ear.

Jim's eyes softened. "This belonged to my daughter. She loved to write stories, just like you."

💀 💀 💀

The students said goodbye to Audrey and boarded the bus to Albuquerque. Amanda sat beside Ms. Bowler.

"Did you enjoy the trip, Amanda?"

"I sure did, even though there was more about ghosts than I would have liked. I'm worried about Cleo though. Some people say she's crazy. She seems obsessed with ghosts. I still can't believe they exist. Do you?"

The teacher thought for a minute. "I think it doesn't matter. It's whatever you want to believe. If you believe there are ghosts, then there are. If you don't, then there aren't. Some people claim to see spirits and ghosts, and perhaps they do." She patted Amanda's hand. "As for Cleo, she has many challenges to deal with, but she is not crazy. You have been a good friend to her on this trip. She needs that. Maybe you could write a story about her, with a happy ending."

Amanda's face lit up. "Yes, that's what I'll do!"

From a couple of rows back Caleb shouted, "Hey, Amanda! Where will you be going to next?"

Amanda turned around and beamed. "I'm not sure, but my friend, Leah, is begging me to come to Holland and see the tulips with her."

"There probably won't be any ghosts there." Caleb winked.

Amanda's cheeks turned red. "I sure hope not."

DISCUSSION QUESTIONS

1. Why do you think Cleo is so anxious and unhappy?

2. Why does Cleo think the ghost of the girl wants to tell her something?

3. Is Jim really a mean person?

4. What do you think Caleb captured on his camera in the gambling room at the St. James Hotel?

5. Have you heard of Wyatt Earp, Kit Carsen, or Annie Oakley before?

6. Does Amanda get in trouble on purpose?

7. Do you think there are such things as ghosts?

8. Would you enjoy a class trip like the one Amanda and her classmates went on?

ACKNOWLEDGEMENTS

I would like to express my sincere gratitude to those who assisted me throughout the writing of this story. To the awesome writers in my critique group, Marion Isberg, Yvonne Pont and Cyndy Greeno who stuck with me every step of the way, giving me honest critiques, suggestions and reasons to continue, I am eternally grateful. To Donna Cluff, my travel buddy, soul mate and friend since birth, thank you so much for coming with me on this adventure and for checking the story for facts. Thank you to horror writer Tausha Johnson who beta read the book and advised on the scary parts. This book would not be a reality without the hard work and meticulous eye of my editor, Michelle Halket of Central Avenue Publishing, to whom I owe a huge thank you. I would also like to thank the wonderful people at the Taos Pueblo who welcomed me and kindly shared their way of life.

Thanks to my parents for encouraging me to be open to all possibilities, to my children who believe in me and to my dear husband for giving me the space to do my scribblings. Thank you to the devoted Amanda Ross followers who have gone with her on all her adventures and keep asking for more. You are the reason I write.

Although the places in this book are real, the characters and events come solely from my imagination. Any factual errors are my own.

The next book in the Amanda
Travels series...

AMANDA
IN
HOLLAND
MISSING IN ACTION

"Who is that boy?" asked Amanda.

Her great-aunt adjusted her glasses and squinted at the faded black and white photograph in the battered album. "That is my oldest brother, Harold." She placed a wrinkled hand on her heart and glanced away. "I believe he was sixteen in that picture. Let me see, yes, it was just before he joined the army."

"You mean he was in the war?"

"Yes, he was in World War II. Harold was so excited to join up he lied about his age." A tear rolled down Great-Aunt Mary's cheek. "But, he never came back. Missing in action was what they told our parents." She sighed. "I still miss him after all these years."

"That's so sad. I didn't know anyone in our family had been in the war. We've been learning about twentieth century wars at school." Amanda looked at the picture again. "Is that his dog beside him?"

"Yes, that was Joey, his Cocker spaniel. Joey was devoted to Harold. He went to the railway station every day waiting for his master, until he passed away seven years later." Aunt Mary had a faraway look.

"Here, you can have this picture." Aunt Mary carefully took the snapshot from the silver corner tabs holding it in place. "Harold had spunk, just like you. And he wanted to see the world. Last time we heard from him, he was in Holland."

"Really? I'm going to Holland to meet my friend, Leah Anderson, from England next week. She wants me to see the tulip fields. You like tulips, don't you, Aunt Mary?"

"Oh, yes. They are my favourite flower. One time Harold saved up his pennies to buy me a tulip for my birthday."

Amanda took one last gulp of tea and brushed her bangs from her eyes. "Thanks so much. I need to get going." She kissed her great-aunt on the cheek.

"Have a wonderful time in Holland. Say hi to Leah from me." Aunt Mary waved from the doorway.

Amanda hung onto the picture of the great-uncle she never got to meet, wondering what he would have been like.

***

Amanda Ross peered up at the tall, colourful houses as she stepped off the curb. The scalloped roofs pierced the sky, making her feel shorter than usual. She didn't notice the bicycle until it was too late.

The woman cyclist swerved to miss her. The bike clattered against the railing. An avalanche of vibrant tulips tumbled from the basket, landing at Amanda's feet.

"*Dombo!*" shouted the woman.

"I'm so sorry." Amanda dropped to her knees and frantically picked up flowers. She held up a white one with red stripes. "This one is so pretty."

"It is called the Canadian tulip. It was created for the one hundred and fiftieth anniversary of Canada."

"Really? I'm from Canada."

"That is very nice, but you really must watch when you cross the street here in Amsterdam. There are many bicycles."

"I am so sorry about that. I'll be more watchful from now on." Amanda lowered a large handful of colourful tulips into the basket attached to the front of the woman's bike.

Something moved at the bottom of the basket.

ABOUT THE AUTHOR

Photo: K. Cullen

Brought up on a ranch in southern Alberta, Darlene Foster dreamt of writing, travelling the world and meeting interesting people. She also believes everyone is capable of making their dreams come true. It's no surprise that she's now the award-winning author of a children's adventure series about a travelling twelve-year-old girl.

A world-traveller herself, Darlene spends her time in Vancouver, Canada and Costa Blanca in Spain with her husband and her amusing dog, Dot.

web: darlenefoster.ca
twitter: @supermegawoman